P9-BYW-472

Kwela
BOOKS
JHANGO
PUBLISHING HOUSE

B M C Kayira

Tremors of the Jungle

Kwela Books

The original watercolour on the cover is reproduced
with the kind permission of the artist, Guiseppe Cattaneo.
This painting, measuring 33 cm x 49 cm, was the basis
for an 18 colour original screenprint produced
at The Caversham Press, KwaZulu-Natal, as part
of the 1995 exhibition "The Spirit of our Stories".
This exhibition combined indigenous
narratives and artists' images.

A Three Continents Book

Published in the United States of America by
Lynne Rienner Publishers, Inc.
1800 30th Street, Boulder, Colorado 80301

ISBN: 0-89410-856-5

Cover design by Lesley Coomer
Set in 11 on 13 pt Monotype Plantin
Printed and bound by National Book Printers,
Drukkery Street, Goodwood, Western Cape
First edition, first printing 1996

ISBN 0-7957-0034-2
KWELA BOOKS, SOUTH AFRICA

ISBN 99908-45-10-7
JHANGO PUBLISHING HOUSE, MALAWI

DEDICATED TO
JEAN-LOUIS JOULIÉ

ONE

The night before a journey has always been a strange night for me. Into that lone night assemble all the related songs of preceding times. Everything has a sound, and everything is a song. And when the rhymes gather, they gather as clouds do before it begins to rain. And there, right there, the clock begins to tick long before the first drop . . .

And sitting here, in this my exile, I remember how that night too was one such night: the night that preceded my return to Fearfong. In that same town, I had spent five years labouring for my Bachelor's Degree, and then for my Honours, at the University of Fearfong. To that same town, to that same University, I was now to return as a member of the University's teaching staff, the thrill of which was so enthralling that it had become a kind of torment.

The night ground on, ground on and groaned – still, the journey ahead, or the prospect thereof, clung to my mind. A particular source of anxiety was the mode by which I was to travel. This same journey, which I had, as a student, made tens of times by bus – skeletal buses too – now I was to make it by . . .

By air!

Yes, by air!

In Manthaland, the Central African country where these events unfold, an aeroplane is something most people can only dream of. Most, indeed, only get close to one when it flies above them once in a while, or when they happen to go to the airport for whatever reason there may be other than flying.

Yet here I was, not just about to see a plane in the skies, but actually about to board one.

It was overwhelming, simply overwhelming. And, tossing in my bed for the millionth time and one, I began to see Fearfong as though I were looking at it from above. Yes, from high up in the air! Of course, from up there, I could see other towns too. I could, for instance, see the sprawling enclave of Timatami, where in fact I was then. I could, also, see the bustling city of Lolagar, the capital of Manthaland, over there in the Central region of the country, some two hundred miles southwards. And then, too, there was that bushy district known as Patichi, far up in the North, where my original home lay. But these places, and all the rest, had just as much meaning for me as the bushes that separated them – which is to say, no meaning whatsoever. They failed to come to life, and they were, at best, a variegated desert from which I had just been rescued. And from that vast desert of sordid existence, Fearfong stood out in mounting significance – stood out high and towered – like the very substance of a dream come true . . .

In the adjoining room, my brother Krom and his wife, whose house this was, had long gone to bed. The entire neighbourhood was in fact all quiet: quiet, hushed up, and still as emptiness. And, for some time yet, I reflected on how easily sleep comes to those who do not court turbulence.

On a rough estimate, it must have been around one in the morning. Presently, I rose up, turned on the lights, and made one last survey of my little room. My belongings, of course, had long been packed away. They were, indeed, few enough to be packed in moments, one and all. But nevertheless I made this last survey, after which I turned off the light and returned to bed. The night grated on; grated on, and still, the journey ahead, or the prospect thereof, clung to my mind.

To be sure, there was much to admire in the career of an academic. Only three months earlier, as a student, I had, like the other students, been earning an allowance to the value of £2 sterling per month. Now, as an Assistant Lecturer, I was to begin earning the unbelievably fabulous sum of £100 a month! I call it unbelievably fabulous because that's what it seemed then. Later, of course, I was to discover that trying to live on that sum was much like trying to walk upside-down up a perpendicular cliff.

For the present, at any rate, I viewed my story as the rags-toriches type. And if that is how I viewed it, my friends and relatives saw even more in it. For them, quite simply, what I had just pulled off was nothing short of a miracle. To them, quite squarely, I, Mati, was a man who, just like that, had managed to drag himself from the mires of a nobody to the crest of a luminous elite. And, of all the privileges that lay in store for me, what they revered most was the prospect of my living in some five-roomed mansion in the lushness and exclusivity of the Tumblefeet Mountains, which towered over Fearfong and dwarfed all else.

For me, however, there was, above all, the prospect of my belonging to a revered academic community. That, as I saw it, was the apex of it all. As a student, I had always marvelled at the depth of perception of some of our lecturers. And I always lived in awe of one of them in particular: an Englishman known only as Professor Chiselwood.

This was the man who, throughout my student days, had astounded me with his ability to lecture without notes. A lecturer in Psychology by designation, he used to insist that, in full, he was a lecturer in the Universal. All the numerous disciplines, so his argument ran, were but wilful considerations of one and the same Universe. The argument continues thus: that an apple, for instance, is Biology, Physics, Chemistry, Mathematics, Religion, Literature, Psychology, Politics – one and all – depending on which angle you choose to view it from. In terms of Physics, it is a solid with a particular shape. In Chemistry, it is a substance whose chemical composition is dominated by water. To the mathematician, it is a single item, to be represented by a number such as 1, or a symbol such as b. To the student of Religion, it is the very fruit the exchange of which led to the fall of Eden. From a literary angle, the search for an apple could constitute, for instance, the centre of a short story, or even a novel. And so on.

Views like these never failed to appeal to my fuzzy mind. Nor was I alone in this regard. In fact, Professor Chiselwood's classes were each like a huge conference. Scores of students – sometimes even folks from outside the University community

– always came and filled the classes of Professor Chiselwood.

Trouble, of course, flared up now and again – when certain students deserted their scheduled classes to attend those of Chiselwood. Or when, alarmed by the man's popularity, the authorities wanted to know what in the name of security was going on on Campus. But we, as students, would no doubt have paid our very last pound just to meet Chiselwood beyond the bounds of Campus. Only, such shows of intimacy between lecturers and students were not at all encouraged by the authorities. It was a standing rule – a sitting rule, even – that lecturers and students should not commune beyond the delimitations of the class-room.

And suddenly, here I was returning to the same Campus, no longer subject to this most peculiar of rules. It was plain and amazing: I would now have limitless access to the likes of Professor Chiselwood!

I had spent three of my five university years with Professor Chiselwood. But only, of course, within the confines of the classroom. Would he welcome me in a private capacity, or would he not?

The night ground on, ground on and moaned. Still, the journey ahead, or the prospect thereof, clung to my mind. The flight was at ten o'clock. And, unless my brother came to wake me up, the possibility was increasing that I would oversleep and miss the plane. Which, quite simply, would have been the exact equivalent of burning one's own house. Or, more exactly still, building a multi-storey building, only subsequently to blast it to debris.

It is at that point, I think, that the scene shifted to a multi-storey building I had never seen before. Some children, it seemed, were clinging to the surface of the skyscraper, screaming for rescue. As for me, I was at the foot of a denuded mountain, in the company of scores of men none of whom I knew. We had been making irrigation-canals on the side of the mountain, which was now but a street away from, and opposite, the skyscraper. As the cries of the children continued, a number of men, who had been working farther up the mountain, came running down with a ladder. And all too soon, the rest of us had grabbed the ladder, and were rushing with it towards the building. Meanwhile, the street in between, previously a tarred one, had turned into a deep, muddy gully, making crossing difficult.

I did not notice how we managed to cross it, or even that we did manage to cross it. I suddenly found myself alone, high on the steps of the ladder, now positioned against the building. The trapped children were nowhere to be rescued. Then, from down there, my fellow workers began withdrawing the ladder.

What?

I tried to shout at them, to tell them to stop. But somehow, my voice couldn't carry. And in the meantime, too, the ladder was no longer leaning against the skyscraper, but swaying dangerously in thin air.

Next, I found myself standing on a balcony of the same skyscraper, from which I could now see that the ladder had been withdrawn. Where the balcony had come from, that I couldn't establish.

I had to find a way of getting to the ground. Looking around, I saw that in the building, there was no room served by this balcony. At best, then, the balcony was like a nest at the tip of a branch in some tall, gigantic tree, from which the only escape would be a dive into the air.

It would have been futile now to shout for help. The skyscraper had changed into some even more gigantic structure, reaching hundreds of miles into the sky. Round and round that dizzying structure I ran, having been joined by a little boy whom I recognised as one of my little brothers. And, together, we dropped from one landing onto the next – until, suddenly, we were dropping through thin air, just like any falling object.

It was one long, nerve-shattering fall. As it went on, I came to discover that my brother was no longer with me. Where he had gone I had not the slightest clue. But somewhere far below, on the ground, I began to see what looked like a lake. It was indeed a lake. Only, I wasn't falling towards it. No. I was, instead, falling towards a burnt knoll only vaguely recognisable. And there someone was standing alone waiting to catch me before I could hit the ground.

I was approaching the ground, approaching all the time, until I caught a branch which somehow projected into my line of descent. The branch broke off, but at that very moment, I heard someone shouting, "Mati! Wake up! It's almost eight o'clock."

Raising my torso with a jerk, I saw my brother standing in the doorway. Slowly, quite slowly, I awoke to the realisation that I was only in my bed, and that the skyscraper-story had been nothing but a dream.

TWO

I was the last passenger to get onto the plane. And no sooner had I stepped in than the sign FASTEN YOUR SEAT-BELT flickered on the panels overhanging the gangway.

It was confusing, being on a plane for the first time ever. Up and down the cabin, the air was rife with the clicks of seat-belts, as the stewardesses moved up and down the gangway making last-minute checks. Presently, one of them came up to me, and asked if the handbag on the floor, stuffed between my legs, was mine. I said it was. Whereupon, she opened the closet immediately above my head, lifted my handbag, and locked it away.

Outside, on the vast stretch of tarmac, tractors were with-drawing from the aeroplane, towing trailers away. And I saw that one of them was actually trailing that very staircase we had used to board the plane. Inside here, the faint hissing of the engines could be heard.

When all the bustle was over, a man's voice burst over the intercom, calling on the cabin crew to check that the doors were locked. As the stewardesses complied, the hissing of the engines picked up momentum, to such a level that one could feel the fuselage vibrating with rebellion. Again, the captain's voice came over the intercom, greeting us all, and giving us details concerning the flight, such as the estimated flight time and the cruising altitude. Finally, the voice went through a list of emergency measures. And as these measures were being read out, the stewardesses, positioned at various points along the gangway, acted them out with an impressive show of co-ordination. The engines became even more delirious, and the vibrations almost ticklish. The voice came on yet again, this time to bid the stewardesses to take their seats, and to an-nounce to us all that take-off was only moments away.

Immediately, the plane started taxiing ahead. It proceeded

slowly, quite slowly, as though encumbered by its own weight. And as it moved, the small terminal building, hitherto blocked from my sight, now swung into view. There, on the balcony, those who had accompanied passengers were waving at us. Due to the hurry of my departure, neither my brother nor his wife had accompanied me to the airport. The hurry, in fact, had even deprived me of the chance to take a bath. And what with the running to the bus stop, and the weight of the suitcase and handbag, I now felt just as though I was emerging from a gym.

We had come to the main section of the runway. Here, the plane came to a halt, as if to do some thinking. The engines began to whistle quite irritatingly, with a numbing vibration running down the fuselage. Moments later, the plane uprooted itself as though it had been startled. And it began racing along the tarmac at ever-increasing speed.

Then, for a moment, such an elusive moment, the plane felt lighter, a trifle lighter. And the next thing, I realised that we were already at an angle to the ground.

So there we were, climbing slowly, battling with the current – like some giant fish struggling to rise to the surface of a vast pool.

I could hardly take my eyes off the scenes below, stretching my neck past the elderly lady who was my seat-mate.

"Do you wish to change seats?" she ended up asking.

"Yes – thank you!" said I, undoing my seat-belt.

By this exchange, I had procured myself the coveted privilege of a window-seat, and was now savouring the awesome beauty of the landscape below.

Later, when we had attained cruising-altitude and were flying above the clouds, the elderly lady said, "Imagine – flying above the clouds!"

"Quite strange, isn't it?" I replied. There was a bout of silence, before I added, "Such that, if it started raining, we would then be flying above the rain, would we not?"

"That's what it means," said the elderly lady, bursting into a laugh.

Out there, the clouds spread out in a continuous sea of white, exuding the impression of one vast valley laden with snow, as I have got to know it here, in this my exile. In places, however, the clouds piled up to form knolls of all shapes, but mostly of the shape of an anvil. In yet other places, the clouds released hold of one another. And in such places, the void far below became visible in a haze of blueness – like patches of sea in a snow-encumbered valley.

We went on flying – flying on and on – as though there really would be no end to it. Yet, during all that time, one never once felt any forward motion; or, particularly, that we were moving at the prodigious speed announced over the intercom. The jerks of the fuselage, were a thing of the past, and all there was now was this evasive passing-by of snow-white clouds. The final effect was of some vague motion effected on the same spot, whatever that may mean. And through this stagnancy, the monotonous drone of the engines, itself almost imperceptible, came as though from quite another world, only distantly related to us. Later, when the stewardesses began serving lunch from a trolley, I ordered myself a beer. And then another. And then another.

From then on, my thoughts seemed to settle on one particular subject: Technology. There was little else so certain of its own self. Of course, man had asserted himself as an enterprising being in many ways. But nowhere, it seemed, was that spirit more evident than in the field of machinery. Here, particularly, the element of courage came to perch itself on that of sheer enterprise. It was marvellous, of course, to make a machine that worked. It was always marvellous. But to make one on whose sole integrity depended the lives of hundreds of people, that, one thinks, is more than just "marvellous". It spells courage – an infinite dose of it – fuelled no doubt by the element of faith. And so there we were, hundreds and hundreds of us, entrusting our lives to the presumed perfection of plane and pilot.

Yet, at the same time, what would man be if he didn't have even a single grain of faith or courage? Everything, even a toddler's first step, has as a prerequisite the banishment of fear. Everything. And so moments of courage really are none other than those when fear is banished wholly. Was it possible, though, to banish fear wholly at one and at all times? Could one . . .

"You must be thinking deeply!" the elderly lady suddenly said.

"It's the beer, I guess," I said, laughing, hailing a stewardess, and calling for another beer.

"It's a strange thing, this alcohol," said the elderly lady. She was, herself, drinking something from a diminutive bottle more particular to lotions.

"It is indeed strange," I replied. "It's probably the fastest river to the sea of bankruptcy!"

Laughing, the elderly lady said, "It may well be. Yet some need a shot of it to build entire financial empires."

"Yes, but only if the shot misses!"

We continued talking along these lines. In the meantime, a queue was slowly forming at the rear of the plane, at the entrance to the washroom. And it then occurred to me that I too needed to visit the washroom. The prospect of queuing, however, rendered the idea rather repulsive. So I chose, instead, to visit the pilot's cockpit.

Through one of the stewardesses, I obtained permission to do just that. And on arrival in the cockpit, I was immediately slapped with awe and amazement at the complexity of the dashboard. Buttons, knobs, dials, levers, dozens upon dozens of glowing little lights. All these lay haphazardly crammed all over the little chamber – save for the space taken up by the windscreen, and the space where the two pilots sat.

Standing behind the two men, I could hardly even think what question to ask. But looking up and smiling, the man on the right said, "Never been to the cockpit before?"

"No!" I exclaimed. "My first time on a plane, matter of fact."

"Oh well, it does become quite boring, eventually," remarked the same man.

The man on the left laughed briefly. What fortified me,

presently, was the relaxed, casual air that hung about these men. The one on the right had some esoteric map spread across his lap. Once in a while, he would lean over to adjust some knob or other, only to return to the map with that same detached, pensive concentration. The other one, the one on the left, just sat there staring at the carpet of clouds ahead, his left leg planted on some kind of platform, his left elbow coming to rest on his thigh in a placid pose.

You would never have thought that our lives, and their lives too, lay entirely in their hands.

I went on to ask a few questions, pertaining to our present speed, to the automatic pilot, and such like. But on the whole, I retained the quietude of these two men who held our fate, the same bizarre sensation of moving-without-moving, and, ahead, that vast stretch of snow where we could just as well have landed.

Later, when I had resettled in my seat, I recounted to the elderly lady how it had all gone, whereupon she remarked, "I would never dream of going in there. It's frightful enough just to be on the plane!"

I thought about that for some time thereafter; about Professor Chiselwood; about that morning's dream; thought back and forth, emptying a good two more beers in the process – until the FASTEN YOUR SEAT-BELT sign flickered on again, and a no longer anonymous voice came over the intercom to announce that soon, we would be landing at Fearfong Airport.

The bumps resumed, plunging the plane yet again into the same wriggle-balance: that frightful, unsettling, yet quite sensuous movement that had followed take-off. And looking through the window, I saw that we were flying right within the clouds. It was difficult to accept that that previously neat, flat, solid carpet of cloud should have turned into this vaporous, impalpable mist now sailing past us. But it all took the mind back to those cold mornings of June when, way back in Patichi, we used to walk to school at six in the morning, clad in shorts and short sleeves, and wholly unshod.

The flaps of the wings, which I had spent some time watching after take-off, were out again. In and out of the main wing they slid, in response, it seemed, to either the turbulence, or the absence thereof. And then, for the first time ever, I noticed a green light at the end of the main wing, flashing on and off without respite, like the warning-signal of some distant lighthouse.

We had emerged out of the clouds – rather, out of the thicket of mist – and we were now floating in an utter void. Beneath us, land was visible again. Yes, land! Twice or thrice, we flew over lower, scantier patches of cloud, whose shadows on the ground, far below, were quite clearly defined: like jagged islands in a sea of brownness.

We kept on descending, kept on wriggling, the weight of the plane asserting itself more and more. I had knocked off, in all, no fewer than seven lagers. A feeling of staleness, topped with the buzz of a headache, now pervaded my entire being. Then, as always, there was the regret of ever having drunk, accompanied by the longing for the now unattainable state of the wholeness of sobriety.

The ground was coming up against us, getting closer by the moment – in the stable instability of the realm of dreams. It was ground, however, such as I had always known it. No longer divided into patches as seen from up there; no longer cast into deliberate, geometrical patterns, but ground as I had always known it: trees, land, buildings, people.

Then, in yet another elusive moment of fleeting lightness, there was a momentary thud, and the next thing, the plane was racing on the ground with that same rumble of wheels and crashing heaviness that had attended take-off.

Home, sweet home!

The plane was being braked gradually, with such effort as made it feel heavier than ever. It did, however, come to a casual, taxiing pace – the same pace with which it had joined the main section of the runway before take-off. At a still slower pace, it took an elaborate turn, and came to a standstill facing the direction from which we had landed.

The terminal building was now visible. Smaller, and far more rural than I could ever have imagined, it had huge, round, golden letters stuck to its façade half-way up its height, reading:

WELCOME TO FEARFONG.

THREE

I was booked in a hotel "pending the allocation of permanent accommodation".

This, in fact, was a matter of procedure. Since a long time before, all freshly recruited academic staff of the University of Fearfong had to begin with a stint at the Testingtime Hotel. The stint over, they were allocated permanent accommodation either on the coveted mountainside of the Tumblefeet Mountains, or in the houses and flats farther below.

The Testingtime Hotel was itself located on the mountainside, just below the mansions, and just above the houses and flats. For that very reason, I suppose, it was generally deemed classy, unique, and on the romantic side of things. Comprising a number of dwarfish, mossy, one-storey buildings, it left one with the impression of a conglomeration of private residential units poised on the terraces. From here, one could see the Campus some two kilometres farther below – beyond which the valley went rolling, farther and farther to where it became Lake McSilence.

At the reception, as I was booking in, I was joined by a young man known as Jah Kalusane. He was, like myself and some eight or ten others, a fresh recruit into the teaching staff of the University of Fearfong. We had done the entire five years of studying together, Jah and I. We had, in fact, pursued more or less the same courses, going "separate" ways only in the final two years, when he went into Sociology, and I into Literature. "Welcome aboard!" Jah now concluded our spell of greetings.

"Thanks!" said I.

"I'll show you to your room," he went on, getting hold of my handbag. "It turns out that your room is next to mine."

"Oh really?"

"You're in 17, ain't you?"

I checked my key holder, and said, "Yep!"

"And I'm in 16."

"You've been here long?"

"Yah! One week to the day."

We went up a series of open-air steps, through two passages, round two separate blocks, and we were now heading for yet another set of steps leading to yet another detached block.

"Quite an ascent, isn't it?" I said, transferring the suitcase from one hand to the other.

"Absolutely interminable," Jah replied.

As soon as we had reached my room, and put the luggage down, Jah said, "I reckon I should give you time to brush it off."

"Thanks, Jah."

"I shall be putting together some notes next door," he added, stepping out.

"Oh the notes!" I exclaimed.

"The notes, yah! One of the less harmless occupational hazards," he laughed.

When he had left, I removed my jacket, hung it on the chair, and then proceeded to undo my tie and shoes. I turned on the in-built radio, and sat on the bed, facing the bathroom.

It was a room more or less as I had imagined it – bed, mosquito net, bedside-table, telephone, wardrobe, bare parquet floor, one and all. From the window, one could see many sections of the hotel, as they slopped out towards the reception. From the bathroom window, one could see, far below, a closely-knit pattern of particularly ancient buildings, squeezed as they were within a formation of bamboo trees.

I plugged the bathtub, and turned the taps on. Then, while the bathtub was filling up, I walked back to the bedroom and lifted the receiver in spite of myself. From the jacket next to me, I pulled out my diary, located Professor Chiselwood's number, and began dialling. As I did so, I noticed that my fingers were in the grip of a slight tremor. Would Professor Chiselwood be at home? Would he accept the fact that my student days were over, that I could now phone him?

In the years that I had been one of Chiselwood's students, I had heard him, on more than one occasion, speak openly in favour of more communion between lecturers and students. Still, one could never be too certain about these things. It could be that . . .

The line opened up, and then: "Hello!"

It was a woman's voice.

"Hello, could I speak to Professor Chiselwood, please?" said I, my heartbeat chaotic.

"Hold on a moment," said the female voice.

I could hear her putting the receiver down.

Was it true or not?

"Hello, Chiselwood speaking."

Really?

"Hello, Prof! It's Mati, here. I was a student of yours for three years, and . . ."

"And you've now joined the Department of Comparative Literature to lecture Creative Writing, and you're calling from the Testingtime Hotel – not so, Mati?"

How . . . How did he know all that?

"Hello, are you there, Mati?" Chiselwood continued, laughing. "Well, there you are! Now, tell me, can I see you this afternoon?"

Could he what when?

"Of course, Prof!" I said, the diary slipping out of my hand. "Just the time it takes for a bath, and I shall be ready!"

"Fine. I shall be there in . . . in . . . let's say an hour's time. Is that all right, Mati?"

"Quite so, Prof!"

"And – call me Chi, will you?"

"All right, Pro . . . er . . . Chi!"

There was laughter at both ends. In the background, I heard the female voice saying something, but I couldn't make out what.

"OK, Mati," Chi finally said. "Meet you at the reception, OK?"

"Thanks, Chi!"

We cut the line. Then, flying to the bathroom, I shed my clothes in less time than it takes to peel a ripe orange, stepped into the bathtub, and . . . I was out of the bathroom long before they had finished reading a five-minute news bulletin on the radio.

About half an hour later, I knocked on Jah's door, and found him reading.

"Gee, you look pretty trimmed up, now!" he observed.

"Thanks, Jah," I said, wondering what I must have looked like before taking the bath.

"Right. Well, I figure it's time to go grazing now." Then, looking at his watch, he announced, "Ten facing two!"

I laughed. His way of telling time had always intrigued me.

"In fact, Jah," I said, "I can only accompany you to the restaurant. I haven't quite the appetite, you know," I went on, drumming my belly.

"What the heck!" he exclaimed, dropping his pen on the dressing table. "On your first day at Testingtime Hotel, you haven't quite the appetite?"

"It must have something to do with my taste buds, Jah."

"I see," he said slowly. "Stale taste buds at Testingtime Hotel!"

I laughed, closing the door in the process.

"Well, besides, I have to meet Professor Chiselwood in less than half an hour's time."

"Whaaat?"

"I mean, I have an appointment . . ."

"On your first day at Testingtime Hotel, you want to meet Professor Chiselwood?"

"Yah. Fine food first needs Chiselwood!" I tried to quip in turn.

"Well, it's up to you, I suppose," Jah mused, rising, pacing about the room, and entering the bathroom. "But Chiselwood is one fellow I sure wouldn't like to be seen standing next to." he added once he had re-emerged.

I laughed.

"It's all up to you, Mati," he went on, putting on his jacket.

As we walked down towards the reception, we saw a woman opening one of the rooms, several blocks downwards. It was . . . It was that elderly woman who had been my seat-mate on the plane!

"Fancy seeing you here!" I called out across the lawn.

She turned around, then said, "Oh, it's you!"

In the meantime, Jah had begun pacing away towards the reception, and had soon vanished.

"It's strange how people always meet," the elderly lady was saying.

"Certainly!" said I. "Are you here for long?"

"No," she answered. "I just passed by to fetch my husband, and then we're off to Lolagar, tomorrow morning. And what brings you here?"

"I shall be working here, and I'm lodged here till I get my own accommodation."

"Oh, good for you, good for you! There is nothing better than free accommodation!"

I laughed, said goodbye to her, and pursued my way towards the reception.

FOUR

I got to the reception at ten minutes after two. Which meant that I had ten minutes to wait – ten minutes before Chiselwood arrived.

As I lowered myself onto the couch, I noticed the receptionist eyeing me in some curious manner, and I said to her, "Excuse me, what time do they stop serving lunch?"

"Three o'clock, sir," she said, almost before I had finished asking. "So you're from Timatami?" she added, examining her fingers.

"Yes I am," said I. "How do you know that?"

"I saw it on your luggage-tag," she answered, still examining her fingers, and smiling like sunshine.

Just then the switchboard began beeping, and, saying "Excuse me" hastily, the receptionist sat down and attended to the switchboard.

Seven minutes to go.

"Your surname suggests you're not from Timatami, though," the receptionist resumed, once she had resurfaced.

"I was born in Patichi," I said, "and that's where my parents are."

"Patichi? Way up North?"

"Way up North! Ever been there?"

"Yes, I, too, come from there."

"Would you like to go back there, some day?"

"Unh . . . Maybe!" she said, with a brief flick of the head, followed by laughter.

Although I could see her only from bust upwards, I could see that she fitted softly into my concept of beauty: those milky-white eyes, that spotlessly smooth face, those fragile, dainty arms sloping smoothly down to familiar landscapes . . .

Four minutes to go.

The porter staggered in just then, bearing two bulky suitcases. Behind him, a man, a woman, and a whole swarm of children. There then followed the interminable process of booking-in, and I stood up.

I spent the remaining moments pacing up and down the car park, exchanging a greeting here, another there. Again, I saw the elderly lady coming down the terraces in the company of a man, whom I supposed to be the husband she had talked of. Then, from down the steep road that shot up from Campus, Chiselwood's green Datsun swerved into the Hotel drive, scaled down the anticline, crunched the gravel of the parking lot – and parked about five metres away from me.

And? And there he was, the man himself!

The driver's door gave way with a grating squeak, and there indeed was Chi himself. Standing almost two metres above the ground, his height seemed enhanced by his shoulder-length blonde mane, as well as his tight jeans. His feet nonetheless were utterly bare, and for a time it looked as though his standing in one spot was due to the fear of the gravel around him. For all that, his face was lit by a smile deep in the bush of his beard – like some kind of aperture in a thicket of bristles. Although this man had been Professor for close to twenty years, he appeared no more than forty.

I walked towards him rather uncertainly, and, smiling, took his extended hand.

"Well, my friend, welcome aboard," he intoned, patting me on the shoulder.

"Thanks, Prof!"

"Chi!"

"Oh, thanks, Chi," I said. "It's this sudden change, Chi!"

"Change? What are you talking about?" he asked, that boyish smile vanishing for a while.

"I mean this sudden transition from being a student to being an Assistant Lecturer."

"Oh come on, Mati. Did you for once believe that sort of distinction?"

"Well, we're in it, Chi, are we not?"

"You've got to be kidding, Mati," he said, laughing, shaking his head. "Well . . . let me just say 'welcome', Mati."

"Thanks, Chi. I am . . . I am . . . I'm glad to be with you – that's about all I can manage, just now."

"Good. Let's go over to my place. How's that?"

"That's fine."

We both laughed; and as we laughed, another car swung into the hotel drive. Its driver was Dr Dush Dush, Head of the Physics Department.

"Afternoon, Prof," said Dr Dush Dush, as he emerged from his car.

"Afternoon," Chi said, signalling me to get into his car.

After we had both got into the car, and Chi was reversing it, he said, "You must have a lot to say about the holidays, I expect."

"Not much, I'm afraid!" said I, repositioning some beer bottles which cluttered the floor of the car. "Just the usual anxiety about the exam results."

We had now reached the intersection with the road that shot up from Campus into the Tumblefeet Mountains. We had come to a standstill, waiting for the traffic to clear. Chi's car was idling uneasily, always trying to go backwards down the slope, and the engine threatening to go dead. Directly opposite us, the Parliament Buildings loomed in their eternal slumber. To the right, the Tumblefeet Mountains towered high into the heavens, the narrow, tarred road snaking into them as though by decree.

Far from going uphill towards the mansions, he started going downhill, in the direction of Campus.

He glanced at me, strayed into the other lane as he did so – then steered the car back to course.

We sped past the Post Office on the right, the Electricity Supply Commission offices on the left, and so on and so forth, till, far downhill, we reached the junction with Kham Kham Highway – the only "highway" in the entire country.

Now that we were facing downhill, Chi's car was idling with a little more ease, as car after car sped from up and down the

Highway. The town of Fearlong lay uphill, some two kilometres to our right. To our left the Highway led downhill to Lolagar, some one hundred kilometres northwards. Down the slope began the flats and houses of those lecturers who couldn't be contained on the sides of the Tumblefeet Mountains.

Presently, Chi depressed the car's cigarette lighter, fumbled for his cigarettes, extricated them from his jeans, popped out two and extended the packet in my direction.

"No, thanks!" I said.

"You don't smoke, is that it?"

"I don't smoke, Chi."

"Lucky young man!" he observed, pulling out one cigarette with his teeth and lighting it.

We took off yet again and to my surprise, we started racing down the Highway – in the direction of Lolagar. I had expected that Chi would live on the slopes of the Mountain, along with all the other University teaching staff.

FIVE

I resolved to ask where we were going. As I was about to do so, however, I found myself asking about something else.

"Say, Chi, how did you know I was at Testingtime Hotel; and how is it that you know the rest of the story?"

Chi looked at me in that same curious manner, then, puffing at his cigarette, said, "Well, let's say I'll tell you later."

I was surprised at how much he could imitate my voice. But while I marvelled, he was busy laughing and dragging on his cigarette – and I ended up laughing along.

"Well," he resumed, on a more serious note. "Fearfong is a small place, Mati."

Chi drew on his cigarette, shook the ash straight onto the car floor, shifting gear at the same time.

We crossed the Kukuluzi River, which tumbled down from the Tumblefeet Mountains on the left, and started going up a steep slope. On the right, across the river, the Campus was now visible, its orange-red bricks peeping through the blue-gums that guarded this portion of the Highway. In the other direction the Mountains blocked the horizon, as they had always done in ages gone by.

A lorry precariously loaded with timber was now ahead of us. It groaned and purred, scarcely making headway, ejecting gusts of soot enough to outrage any environmentalist. And this was a two-lane "highway", so at an incline like this, it would be difficult to overtake the lorry.

"It's a long story, Mati," Chi resumed, winding up the driver's window. "But to begin with, I should tell you that I'm on the University's Appointments Committee."

"I see!" said I, winding up the window on my side.

"And, take it from me, it was a battle getting you appointed," he went on, flicking the indicator, engaging first gear and shooting ahead to overtake the lorry.

The forest of bluegums on the right had now come to an end. The Campus was visible without the slightest obstruction, its buildings encrusted into the slope, densely arranged at the top, and thinning out towards the plain below. At the lowest end was the Campus's Tidzadzuka Stadium, plumb in the centre of a forest of young pines. Beyond this forest began the little villages of thatch and mud – and so the plain spread out down to where it became Lake McSilence.

"It was a battle, you say?" I asked.

"A real brazen battle, I tell you. Virtually everyone on the Committee was disinclined to appoint you – you and Vivi."

"Vivi? Has he been appointed in the Law Department?"

"Yes, indeed."

Thinking of Vivi, I began laughing. "But on what grounds were they disinclined, Chi?" I asked.

"That's the point – on the grounds that you two know nothing about decorum!"

I wound down the window on my side.

"My argument," Chi went on, "was that it would be shameful if a university recruited its teaching staff on any consideration other than the academic. Whereupon, one of them stood up and shouted: What the hell! What these two chaps deserve is a public flogging, not an appointment!"

I exploded with laughter. Ahead, the cars raced on their way towards Fearfong, or, beyond Fearfong, the little industrial town peculiarly named Scotland, some forty kilometres southwards.

We went past Zazan Inn, past Jombo Night Club – both of them spots where many students from Campus, myself included, spent more time than on Campus. We sped on – past the junction to Fearfong Airport, past Zazan Fishing Flies. On both sides of the Highway, the land had taken on its eternally rural aspect: dry maize gardens, scorched grass, thatch dwellings – one and all.

"Well, looks like I owe you quite a bit!" I said.

"A whole herd of cattle, in fact."

We laughed.

"By the way, did you go up North, over the holidays?" Chi went on.

The North of Manthaland is where virtually all its cattle come from, thousands of which are carted southwards daily to areas like Fearfong. And for each beast, the former owners, deep in the bush of the North, are paid roughly the price of a pair of sandals, maybe even less.

"Oh yah, I did go, Chi. In fact, I only came down to Timatami less than a month ago."

"To await the verdict closer to the source, I suppose?"

"No, to await the source closer to the verdict!"

"I see . . . I see . . ."

We had now reached Kogan, a little, smouldering township of dust, brick and tin, which adorned both sides of Kham Kham Highway. All around, the folk were mingling about: pushing wheelbarrows, pulling goats along, arranging their fruit-stalls, warding flies off their piles of fish, buying and selling amid the avid calls of ardent vendors.

Chi had flicked on the left indicator, and we were slowing down. We soon turned left, indeed – only to find ourselves on a rough, dusty road that plunged right into the heart of Kogan Township. The Tumblefeet Mountains, or their foothills, were now directly ahead, louring in the background like the arch of some ancient monster, running north to south like an endless barricade.

The sun was sinking towards the Tumblefeet, and now the shafts of its rays were directly thrust upon us. We drove on slowly, absorbing the bumps and dust. We waved to the folk out there, still mingling around and laughing. In places, the road narrowed down to but a mere path. You could hear the wheels crunching the bordering bush, the projected twigs scratching the already flaked Datsun. Drift followed drift, corner led to corner. And still, we ploughed on and on towards the Tumblefeet Mountains. From time to time, children yelled, "Chiii! Chiii!" as they waved heatedly and ran after us, danced and capered, putting their hands to the car, and shouting still more.

We eventually entered a yard studded with mango and guava

trees, beneath which grew short, well-tended grass. About ten metres uphill, bordering the yard, stood a house roughly half the size of a netball pitch. It stood lengthwise, like – much farther beyond – the Tumblefeet themselves. Its walls were made of planks of split wood. The roof was thatch, and about halfway down the height of the left side of the façade, a wooden sign lay glued to the wall, whose lettering, in green paint, read: SPLIT WOOD, NOT ATOMS!

We parked right beneath its veranda of earth and stone.

"This is where I nest!" Chi announced, getting out of the car.

For the first time I noticed his sandals, lying as they did next to the car's foot-controls.

As we went up the steps leading to the veranda, the door – itself made of vertically arranged planks – suddenly opened and a woman in her thirties presented herself to sight.

"Hi, Mati," she said, smiling. "Welcome home!"

"Thanks, er . . ." I began.

"Daisy," said she.

"Thanks, Daisy," I responded, as we shook hands.

The veranda, though made of earth, had been so thoroughly scrubbed that it shone almost like a cement floor. Not far off, about ten metres on either side, began other houses. Like Chi's house, they were of wood and thatch. Down the slope, where we had come from, past the Highway far in the eastern plain, Lake McSilence gleamed in its immobility – like a distant puddle glinting in the mud.

"Right, let's step in," Chi said.

We walked into the house.

It was like stepping into some kind of art gallery; a curio-shop, maybe; a museum, even – or, more accurately, a combination of all these. Armchairs and easy chairs, couches and stools made of wood or straw – items of that sort were positioned casually, yet in some kind of pattern, all over the sitting room. Here and there stood tables of various shapes. The seats, for the most part, had straw-stuffed cushions on them. And as I lowered myself onto one of the couches, I was startled by just how much comfort there was in it. The walls were patterned with paintings and drawings; masks and other carvings told their own story. On the cupboard, on the room-divider, various curios were clustered in shapely arrangements, with plants or flowers taking up whatever space was left.

Now and again, an eastern breeze came sweeping in through the many open windows. Searching the ceiling with my glance, I soon discovered that there was nothing here to suggest electricity. And in all this entanglement, the telephone set, positioned on the cupboard, looked rather unbelievable.

"I bet you were expecting a palace of some sort," Chi broke the uneasy silence, as he lowered himself on the couch, next to me.

"Not really, Chi," I said, removing my jacket, and then my tie."It's just that I thought you stayed up on the Mountain."

"He wouldn't!" said Daisy, positioning mugs of earthenware on the table in front of us. "He's afraid of heights, this Chi of yours." Amid that, she disappeared behind the room-divider, only to re-emerge with a bottle of home-made wine.

"Afraid of heights, me?" Chi retorted. "What? I used to be an acrobat, in earlier times."

"At sea-level, yes!" Daisy pursued, filling the mugs with wine.

We all laughed.

"Here!" Chi said, lifting his mug. "To our friendship, all of us!"

We clinked the mugs, and fell to drinking, even as Daisy sat next to Chi.

"I imagine you get robbed quite a lot in this neighbourhood," I began.

"We would be, I suppose," Chi said, lighting a cigarette. "If we had something robbable."

I laughed, more at the word "robbable" than at the theory postulated.

"The car, for instance," I went on, taking another long sip. But just then, a young man in torn jeans and unstrapped sandals walked in through the main door.

"Shall I get the meat, Chi?" he asked, chewing gum.

"Sure," said Chi. "The car-keys are in the ignition."

"Right on!" yapped the young man, affecting an American accent. "Kerma and the others will soon be fixing the fire outside."

"Wonderful!" said Chi. "Oh, Bits, come greet Mati. Mati, this is Bits."

"I know you from long ago," Bits remarked, as we shook hands.

"I've seen you somewhere, too," said I.

"At Zazan Inn, I should imagine," Chi intervened.

As we laughed, Bits turned round and vanished through the main door. Within moments, the car came to life, and drove off.

"He stays in the neighbourhood, does he?" I began, indicating the spot where Bits had been standing.

"He does." Daisy rushed in, swallowing as she did so. "And so do they all, all of them. Believe me, Mati, there're so many of them that you'll never get to master all their names."

"Oooh, never mind her," said Chi, facing me. "She doesn't quite like them, that's what."

"Look, Chi," Daisy railed, "I know I'm African, and I know they're African too. But must I tolerate them walking in and out of here as though it were their own house?"

We all sipped in silence, before Chi said, "And whose house is it, Daisy?"

"Yours, of course."

"Really?"

"He's like that, you know," said Daisy, looking at me rather tearfully.

"When I return to England, will the house still be mine?" Chi probed, looking at Daisy point-blank.

"Listen to him, Mati! I'm talking of who owns the house now, he goes to talk of who will own the house tomorrow!"

"Yah. I mean, why should I be serious about something of only now?"

"And what if you had to stay here forever, Chi?" Daisy pursued.

"Forever? What do you mean, 'forever'?" Chi laughed.

"Well, why did you build the house, in the first place? And why did you buy the car?"

"Daisy, I built the house so that I can sleep in it. I bought the car so that it can facilitate my movements. As simple as that."

"Fine. And yet you cannot admit to owning them," Daisy said.

"Take the air we breathe, Daisy," Chi went on, rather despondently.

"The air we breathe! What does it have to do with any of this?"

"Well, the air is useful to us, is it not?"

"It certainly is!"

"Would you say we own it, for that reason?"

"No. But we don't buy the air, do we?"

"What if it became scarce, and we had to buy it, heh?"

"What do you mean? How can anyone buy air, Chi?"

"How can we buy air? There're things that we buy now which people long ago never bought. Like water. Like firewood. I mean, originally, nothing was ever for sale – was it, Mati?"

"I don't think so," said I.

"That's it, Daisy!" Chi went on. "And some day, when it becomes scarce enough, air may have to be bought."

"Well, with those cigarettes of yours, it may indeed end up becoming scarce," Daisy laughed. "But what are you saying, actually?"

"I'm saying the best and the most we can do is make use of the things nature has put at our disposal. When we're here no longer, others will come and make use of the same things. Not so, Mati?"

"It seems so. Sure!"

"Good," said Chi. "And as for you, Daisy, don't look so glum, because glum gives gloom, and gloom begets granny."

Daisy burst into laughter. And laughing, she sprang off and disappeared behind the room-divider, only to re-emerge with another bottle of home-made wine.

SIX

I woke up the following morning not knowing where I was. Rather than uncover my head, however, I settled on playing a familiar game of mine – retracing the events of the previous night, trying to deduce where I could possibly be. Here we go: Chi's place. The wine. The argument between Chi and Daisy. The barbecue. Dozens and dozens of revellers. The dancing. The talking. The laughing. And then?

And then nothing . . .

I cast off the blankets – only to discover I was at Testingtime Hotel!

After some more thinking, I discovered that today was a Sunday. Yes, a Sunday, one of those days on which finding what to do is far more difficult than doing what you've found.

Meanwhile, snippets from yesterday's party, held in Chi's orchard, kept coming back to my mind. It was a fragmented picture. I remember, for instance, talking to many of the revellers. But about what? That I do not know. I remember, too, talking to Chi at length. But about what? That too I do not know. Bits of information, however, come tumbling my way. Such as the discovery that Chi was a vegetarian; that he had been living with Daisy almost from the very first year of his arrival in Manthaland; that Chi had promised to come and see me on the morrow – and so on. Yet even that comes to my mind as though from another world . . .

In the immediate, I had this problem: just what time was Chi supposed to come and see me? Would he come straight to the room, or was I supposed to wait for him at reception?

I spent long moments trying to piece matters together; tossing beneath the bedding, and, in general, barely surviving the unsparing nausea of the aftermath of revel.

Until I realised it was heading – for midday!

Flinging the linen aside, as well as the edge of the mosquito-net, I darted to the bathroom like a mouse that had had a close shave. But even as I ran, I could feel the throbbing headache, the evasive dizziness, the flattening staleness that made you want to throw up at the very thought of food.

A cold bath, perhaps, was the answer to my present condition. As I turned on the cold-water tap, however, the phone ripped the air with its strident, startling bell – exactly as though it had been timed to go off the same time as the tap.

I rushed out of the bathroom, and, conscious of my nudity, lifted the receiver. "Hello!" I panted.

"Mati, it's Chi here."

"Oooooh."

"How are you coping with the aftermath?"

If my condition could be called "coping", well . . . "Barely!" I said.

"Same here. That's why I couldn't come at ten, you know."

Had he come at ten, he would have had to deal with a patient, or much worse!

"At ten, Chi?"

"Yep! I was supposed to pick you up at ten, remember?"

Oh no!

"Never mind, Chi. You're talking to one struck with amnesia!"

"Well, that's what life is, my friend: a spell of amnesia which we spend trying to recall where we were before."

I was hardly in the mood for such talk.

"Meanwhile, do you know where your tie and jacket are, Mati?"

I looked around the room, wiping beads of sweat from my brow. "In my wardrobe, I should imagine."

"No, sir, in *my* wardrobe!"

Oh no!

"I've got to quit the bottle, Chi."

He chuckled. And as he did so, I could hear him sipping something.

"What – you're at it again, Chi?"

"Sure, my friend. Fighting fire with fire."

I laughed.

Some moments went by during which nothing was said between us – a bout of silence in which I could hear Daisy dragging the furniture about.

"Mati?"

"Yah?"

"Look, I'll see you at two then, all right? Remember, we're supposed to go to the mountain top."

"In a manner of speaking, remember!"

Chi laughed.

Then I remembered something else, and said, "Wait a minute, Chi."

"Unhuu? Don't tell me you forgot your feet somewhere?"

"No – it's the notes, Chi. I've got to prepare notes for tomorrow."

At which Chi laughed more prolongedly than he had ever done so far.

"What . . . What . . . What?" I tried to break in on his laughter.

"Notes, Mati? Who put that idea into your head?"

"What idea, Chi?"

There was silence.

"Oh well, let's put it this way, Mati, we'll talk about it up the Mountain."

Still, I remained silent. The receiver, meantime, had gathered sweat, and I shifted it to my right hand.

"Mati?"

"Hello!"

"I said don't bother about it. We'll fix it."

Even by the time I emerged from the bathroom, about an hour later, I wasn't anywhere close to understanding Chi's remarks regarding the lecture notes. Professor Chiselwood was, of course, known for conducting his classes without the aid of prepared notes. But that he should expect me to do the same – if that's what he expected me to – that didn't make sense. None whatsoever. In thirty or forty years' time, maybe I, too, would have gained enough experience to teach without prepared notes. Maybe. For the present, not at all.

I changed into fresh clothes, and resolved to call on Jah.

There was no answer from his room.

For a while, I toyed with the idea of returning to my room to work on the notes. Remembering Chi, however, I shelved the idea.

What next, then?

Why, what about a drink in the Hotel's bar, next to the reception?

Why not, indeed?

As I approached the reception, I remembered the receptionist from the North, and our brief, unfinished conversation of the day before.

I stepped into the reception, only to discover that there was a man in place of the female receptionist. A man, in fact, whom I knew by sight for having drunk with him in town, once or twice.

"Say, do we have to leave our room-keys at the reception each time we leave the premises?" I now asked the man.

"That's the rule, yes," said the man. "But you . . . How long are you going to be here?"

"Oh . . . It could be weeks; it could be months . . ."

"Oh well, look, as long as you keep the keys safe, do sneak out with them, whenever necessary," he said, winking. "I mean, it would be tedious to have to collect the keys each time, particularly when you're coming from hunting, and you've got game with you."

"Hunting?"

"Yah, I mean, a man can't sleep alone all the time, can he?"

"Oh, I see!" said I, laughing. "You call it hunting, do you?"

"Yah! It's the only kind of hunting where nobody gets killed, see?"

As I laughed again, I became aware that my sides were aching – either from too little food, or too much alcohol, or both. And I wondered just how much I had eaten yesternight.

I was going out of the reception when the male receptionist suddenly said, "Hey, you're in Room 17, are you not?"

"I am."

The man then turned to the pigeon-holes, swept an envelope out of the one marked "17" and handed it to me.

"Thanks," I said, receiving the envelope.

It was simply marked "Room 17". Putting it into my trouser pocket, I went down the passage, past the restaurant, and so into the bar.

Jah was sitting at the horseshoe counter. Next to him was Chakankonz, a lecturer in Sociology.

"Hello, gentlemen!" said I, sitting next to Chakankonz.

"Hello, Mati!" Chakankonz said. Whereupon Jah resumed talking to Chakankonz, and I ordered a beer.

To my left, two other men were conversing in low tones. As I paid for my beer, I said to the barman, "Why is the beer so drunkenly expensive?"

He did not say anything in return, nor did anyone else.

As the first sip sank down my system, I could literally feel my nerves distending, like the coursing of the initial thrust of water in a hose-pipe. I shuddered furtively from the impact of it, again wondering just how much I had eaten at Chi's place.

I followed up with another sip.

All the while, I had this vague feeling of being observed from the left, but I tried not to pay attention. And presently, the barman turned on the music-system, largely dispelling the tension.

I then reached into my trouser pocket, pulled out the envelope and ripped it open.

Dear Mati,
I'm sorry about yesterday. I shall be
on duty from 3.00 p.m.
Thanks,
Kettie (Receptionist)

As I put the note away, Chakankonz spun around on the rotating stool, and, now facing me, remarked, "The mail is pouring in already, heh?"

"Oh it's just a tiny note," I said, sipping.

On the other side of Chakankonz, Jah was beating a continuous note on the counter, his glance lost somewhere beyond the barman. For a moment, the attention of the men on my left was distracted. And at that very moment, Chakankonz pointed at the two men in swift succession. I nodded.

The music was coming on softly, and the drinking carried on. Later, when the two men on my left had departed, Chakankonz turned to me again, and said, "Come over this side. I have something to whisper to you."

Taking my glass along, I followed Chakankonz to the couch in the farthest corner. As we sat on the couch, Jah, still at the counter, emptied his glass at one go, dropped from the stool – and began walking out of the bar.

"Wait for me, Jah!" Chakankonz called out. "I shan't be long."

"Heh, I got something more important to do, OK?" Jah snapped.

And, with that, he took exit.

For a while, Chakankonz appeared confused. But after taking a sip, he said to me, "Listen, Mati, you have now entered a totally new world, this world of academics."

"Thanks for that!" I said.

"And what it means, basically, is that now you must exercise much more care. See what I mean?"

"Not really."

"Those two men you were sitting next to. Do you know them, for instance?"

"No."

"Do you know what they are?"

"Not until you signalled to me."

"Undercover cops!" he whispered, glancing swiftly at both the door and the barman.

"I got your signal all right," said I, emptying my glass.

"It's a new world, Mati. It's quite another world. From now on, you'll always be shadowed by undercover agents. Always!"

At that moment Vivi appeared in the doorway and looked around.

"Ah, Mati!" he exclaimed as he walked over to our corner. "Welcome back to Fearfong."

Chakankonz had fallen silent.

"Hello, Vivi!" I said, getting up.

Vivi glanced at Chakankonz. "See you later." With a slap on my back he departed.

Chakankonz resumed talking as if Vivi had never made an appearence. I ordered another beer.

"So you must watch what you say, Mati. You complained just now about the price of the beer, in their presence. Remember?"

"And then?"

"Mati, you're not a foreigner, are you? I mean, you know that complaining about prices in this country can get you into trouble, don't you?"

"I do. But I've never understood why."

"Well, it's taken that you're criticising the economic system of the country."

"Fine. And if I complain about what is not working well, am I not in fact helping the system?"

"Mati, are you drunk?"

"Maybe. But I mean, if I pointed out the leaks in your roof, would I not be helping you, for instance?"

And then, for close to a minute, Chakankonz looked deep into my eyes, as if he were trying to peer into my soul.

"Mati, I can't believe it," he said finally, detaching his words. "But by all means, don't draw me into politics. Please!" he added, drinking. "This association of yours with Chiselwood, if I may advise you, is not a safe one."

"What about it?"

"The man has been branded a nonconformist, you know."

"So?"

"In sociological terms, we call him a 'deviant'."

"All right!"

"It means, in effect, that he thinks, talks, and acts differently from the rest of us."

"Well, I'll tell you what, in Literature, we call it 'originality'."

"Mati!"

"I mean, who says everybody should behave like everybody else?"

"Our system doesn't like deviants, as you know. And, if I may divulge something to you, Chiselwood would have been deported long ago, if it wasn't for the fact that he is now a citizen of this country."

"Deported for thinking differently?"

"If the system considers that as subversive, what can you do about it?"

"But how can there be improvements in the system, if thinking is prohibited?"

"Look, the government doesn't like it, that's all."

"Yah, the problem is that the government is running a system of which you and I are part. So . . ."

"All right, Mati," said he, rising to his feet. "At least I have warned you, have I not?"

Oh well!

At exactly two o'clock, Chi's Datsun swang into the parking-lot.

"You're a human clock, Chi!" said I, opening the passenger door.

"That's how friendships start off, Mati – with on-the-dot punctuality. Later, they become on-the-dot punctures!"

I stood there laughing, unable to bend over and get into the car.

"Let's get going, Mati!" Chi urged.

As I got in, I saw my tie and jacket lying on the back seat, and I shook my head silently. We drove off.

SEVEN

Again, we idled at the T-junction beneath the Parliament Buildings. When the road was clear, we swerved, and started going uphill.

We were going straight up the Tumblefeet Mountains. At its lower slopes, we passed the Government Print, the School Certificate Commission, the Censorship Commission, and so on – all of them governmental agencies whose very names told the history of Manthaland.

The Datsun groaned and purred; purred, groaned and squeaked. On the right, at longish intervals, gigantic mansions were now peeping at us from behind the pines – it was the idea of me moving into one of these same mansions one day, that had impressed my friends and relatives so much. On the left, the Mountain plunged down into a fearsome cliff – so fearsome you developed a running stomach just by staring at it too long. And at the bottom of the cliff, far down there, the town of Fearfong appeared, as if through a smoky haze. Cleaving the town like a huge, black snake, Kham Kham Highway gleamed in the afternoon sun, lost in places behind trees and buildings, but gleamed on yet again – farther and farther on its way towards Scotland . . .

"Chi?" I broke the spell of silence.

"Yah?"

"A little while ago, some fellow reminded me it's an act of subversion to complain about rising prices."

"Yep! And it's only just the beginning, Mati."

"So the fellow told me!"

"Subversive, communist, agitator, rebel . . . those are some of the titles that are heaped on me daily."

"And what do you say to it all, Chi?"

"Oh well, my ambition in life is to do what I regard as good," he said, swerving to avoid a jutting branch. "The rest are mere details, as Einstein once said."

"He said so?"

"Yah! He said: My aim is to know God's thoughts. The rest are mere details."

I remained silent, gazing straight ahead at the thread of tarmac that pierced the Mountain.

"Look at it this way, Mati. No human being, no animal, would like to be hurt. Right?"

"Except masochists, Chi!"

"Not even masochists, my friend."

"How is that? I thought masochists delight in being hurt?"

"So we think, Mati. In fact, they derive *pleasure* from those apparently hurtful things."

I remained silent.

"Take this cigarette I'm smoking, for instance."

"Right?"

"People may regard me as a masochist for smoking something which is known to kill. For my part, I smoke it not to harm or kill myself, but to satisfy some desire within me."

"I'm following."

"So even presumed masochists don't wilfully seek to harm themselves, or to be harmed by anyone else. No one ever seeks that."

"OK."

"From which it is easy to see that a commitment to do good is the only ideal there is – or the ideal towards which all ideals tend."

"I'm following."

"And that is why I try to make doing good, or what I regard as good, my ultimate ambition."

"I get it."

"As for trying to topple an evil government, and suchlike, that I'm not foolhardy enough to try."

"What do you mean, Chi?"

"I mean it's futile, Mati. It's like trying to water the leaves, and not the roots, of a plant dying of thirst."

By now, the Mountain was so steep that we were proceeding at almost a walking pace.

"I don't quite follow, Chi."

"The evil government is the drying leaves. The roots are the heart of man."

"I see. Still, evil has to be stamped out, not so?"

"Indeed. But that can only be achieved by the watering of the roots, not the leaves."

"By changing the heart of man, you mean?"

"Exactly so!"

The mansions had now ceased, and thickets of pine trees flourished everywhere.

"I see. But how do you propose to carry out such a gigantic task as changing the heart of man, Chi?"

"By doing good, of course. Wherever possible. I do you good. You do Mr X good. X does to Y. Y does to Z, and so on."

"And then?"

"And then, when everyone has learnt to do good to everyone, where will an evil government come from – outer space?"

The chill was rising, and I wound up the pane on my side.

"I think I understand, Chi. But how long do you think good would take to spread to every person on earth?"

"Less time than a sexually transmitted disease would take."

"How is that?"

"You could do good to hosts of people in a day. But you may not mate with as many!"

I laughed long. And, all of a sudden, the knot of anger I had felt since leaving the bar somehow began to melt. It was a legitimate kind of anger, I had to concede. But then, what isn't legitimate?

The rest of the climb was effected in total silence – total, that is, save for the growling of the engine and the squeaking of the chassis, which pervaded the air all the time.

Suddenly, the ascent had ended, and the next thing, we were rolling on completely flat land.

It was the Tumblefeet Plateau, about which, even as children back in primary school, we used to sing songs of unqualified admiration. And at this point, I wondered briefly how, in all the five years that I had lived in Fearfong, I had never even thought of coming to the Plateau.

Here the grass was short and green, so much so that you would have thought someone tended it, while the trees – brachystegia for the most part – were scanty and dwarfish. Fearfong town was no longer visible, nor was anything else far down there. And in this lofty veld, a single building stood lonely and dejected, with the sign KWABENE INN glued to its façade in still timelessness.

There were no other signs of human habitation anywhere around – just the grass, just the occasional tree, and then this narrow, by now gravel road which meandered past the Inn, into the veld, and far beyond.

We branched off into the drive leading to the Inn, on the right. As we parked at the entrance, I remembered with a wince the note in my pocket:

Dear Mati,
I'm sorry about yesterday. I shall be
on duty from 3.00 p.m.
Thanks,
Kettie (Receptionist)

We got out of the car, exchanged greetings with the man at reception, and continued down the corridor into a spacious, circular bar.

There was no one in the bar, save for the barman, who was busy wiping an array of glasses.

"You OK, Gochi?" Chi greeted, as we took position at the counter.

"Very fine, Chi," said the barman. "It's quite quiet today, heh?"

"Oh well, it's a Sunday, my friend," Chi went on. "Give us two lagers, and drink anything you like, Gochi."

"Righto!" enthused Gochi, getting busy with the drinks.

When the drinks had arrived, and we both had sipped, Chi said, "About the notes, now."

"About the notes, Chi!"

"Do you know, Mati, that logic is merely a difficult word for common sense?"

"It is?"

"It is," said Chi, blowing a jet of smoke across the counter. "It is logic, or common sense, which dictates that when a door is closed, you have to open it to get into the house, or out of the house; that before you smoke a cigarette, you've got to light it first. And so on. Do you follow?"

"Sure."

"Right. In short, the world is made up of rules of common sense. Which implies that if one could follow every rule correctly, there is nothing one could fail to do. Does that make sense?"

"To some point, yah."

"To some point?"

"Yah. I mean, there are so many things that we humans cannot do, Chi. Are there not?"

"I know. But that's only because we don't always follow the rules of common sense. As someone once said, the trouble with common sense is that it's not very common."

"I see."

"I mean it, Mati. I mean, even myself – there are lots and lots of things I cannot do. But that's only because, in those things, or at such times, I lack common sense."

"Fine. But how does that get us to the notes, Chi?"

"We've just established that the rules of common sense apply to everything, have we not?"

"We have."

"Right. Which means even subjects classified as academic are included."

"Oh no, Chi!"

"No?"

"No! Would you have me believe, Chi, that something as complex as Electronics is mere common sense?"

"Why not, Mati? I mean, what's Electronics but the fact that electronic messages are relayed from point A to point B?

What's Engineering but the fact that things must be assembled in such a way that they do not block the flow of energy – or that they do not collapse? What's Mathematics but the fact that things or concepts can be represented by figures? What's Literature but the fact that feelings can be coded into words?"

"In other words, whatever doesn't work lacks common sense?"

"That's it! And it is known, more commonly, as a 'mistake'. Something taken wrongly, in other words. If, for instance, you eat the last two bananas in the house, and still expect them to be there, you're lacking in common sense; you're making a mistake, are you not?"

"Certainly!"

"Unhuu! In mathematical terms, it would be like saying two minus two equals two."

"I see," said I, emptying my glass. As I ordered the next round of drinks, the receptionist turned up to say a few things to the barman. "Get a drink of your choice, too," I said to the receptionist.

"Thanks!" said he. "And I'll have snacks sent to you in a moment."

As the receptionist walked away with his drink, Chi winked at me, and I winked back.

"But what of more complex mathematics, Chi, such as Calculus?" I resumed.

"Complex Mathematics, merely represents in figures or symbols complex thoughts or happenings. If, instead of eating the two bananas, you split them into a thousand pieces, mix them up several times – and then try to determine which piece came from which banana, or which piece you broke in the twentieth second, you will then be in the domain of probability, of Calculus, and so on."

"I see, I see!"

"You remember that quote from Einstein?"

"I want to know . . ."

"I want to know God's thoughts. The rest are mere details."

"Right, right!"

"The universe is but something into which the Creator – the Creative Force, if you prefer – has encoded a myriad laws. And all we're doing, in our various disciplines – even in everyday life – is decoding those laws. Isaac Newton, seeing an apple fall, decoded the law of Gravity. Galileo, peering into the skies, decoded the law that everything rotates around something. A farmer, when it rains too much, decodes the law that too much water is no good for his plants. You, drinking too much, decode the law that too much drinking spoils your appetite. And so on. That's what we're doing, and that's all we're doing, in this world."

"That's all we're doing?"

"That's all we're doing. And obviously, the more laws you discover, the more what you discover is regarded as complex. Hence Calculus. Hence Quantum Physics. Hence Aesthetics. Hence Agriculture. And so on. You know that Einstein also said: We only use ten per cent of our minds?"

"Yah."

"That's it. If you used fifteen per cent of your mind, you would discover five per cent more laws than you would if you used ten per cent. If you used twenty per cent of your mind, you would discover ten per cent more laws, and so on."

"I see. Logically, then, one can go up to using hundred per cent of one's mind?"

"If you could concentrate one hundred per cent, yah! Why not? Except, you can never concentrate one hundred per cent. No, you can't. To achieve that, you would have to reduce distraction to zero. Absolute zero. Which means you would have to be out of your body, out of this world."

"I see, I see. That's probably why we have to wait until we die before we can know everything?"

"I think so too; I think so too!"

"But now, let's come straight to the point, Chi," I resumed, refilling my glass. "Tomorrow, I'm supposed to handle three or four classes in Creative Writing. The way you say it, I walk into class equipped only with a piece of chalk – is that it?"

"Of course."

"And then what?"

"And then the greeting, of course."

"Fine. But where do I begin, in terms of the lesson?"

"By that time, your lesson has already begun."

I kept silent. Then: "I don't know what you mean, Chi."

"You can only begin with what you've begun with, no?"

"Certainly."

"And you've begun with walking into the classroom, right?"

"Yah."

"So you write on the board, thus: *I walked into the classroom, chalk in hand.*"

"OK."

"Then you ask the students if that expresses fully the way you walked in."

"All right."

"Then one of them will probably suggest: *I teetered into the classroom.* Because, being new, as it were, you may probably have been scared, or shy."

"I see it."

"Another one may suggest: *I marched into the classroom.* Because, being brave, or drunk enough, you may have walked in resolutely."

"All right."

"And so on and so forth, till you all find the words that express best your act of walking into the classroom. Then you do the same with the way you greeted them, the way they responded, the way you walked about, or did not walk about – and so on and so forth. And then you tell them: That, ladies and gentlemen, is what Literature is about – matching words with feelings."

And sitting here, in this my exile, with Chi's notes spread out on the table in front of me, I look back on that Sunday and realise that that conversation put me on a course from which I would not deviate again.

EIGHT

Within weeks, my romance with Kettie got off the ground. Our relationship had taken off following that little note she had left me, at reception. Upon returning from the mountain top, I had headed straight for the reception, propelled largely by the effect of drink, but hoping, at the same time, that she didn't end up thinking so.

"Thanks for the note!" had been my first words. "I actually felt like phoning you from up the Mountain."

"Really? So you've just come back from Kwabene Inn, have you?" she had asked, looking at me rather too fixedly for my comfort.

"Good guess. They have a kind of air up there that tends to purify the sentiments!"

"Quite so. You needed a bit of it, did you not?"

"In order to start anew, yes."

She was silent for some time.

"In order to start anew?"

"Yes, madam! Need I specify who I'm starting with?"

She tried to suppress a smile, but it ended up getting the better of her. "Maybe you should!" said she, smiling.

"Fine. Er . . . She is one with a dimple on either cheek . . ."

"All right!"

"She has soft, bobby hair that makes you want to touch it . . ."

"All right!"

"When she says 'All right!' you feel like kissing her, except you're a little drunk."

She began laughing and, laughing, she went to attend to the switchboard.

We had talked about other things; and, after quite a few interruptions from the switchboard, we had arranged an out-of-the-premises appointment for the following day. And within a few days, we had been to Conetsanthu Hotel; strolled up and down the golf pitch, and watched a memorable presentation of Athol Fugard's *The Blood Knot*.

Within weeks, my classes were drawing unusual numbers of students. Nowhere near as unusual as Chi's classes, to be sure. But quite alarming, all the same. From one class to the next, the numbers increased. Eight, one time; fifteen, the next; twenty, one time; thirty, the next. And so on.

I had taken Chi's hints quite seriously. On the very first day, we had, indeed, explored my act of walking into the classroom, as well as what had followed that particular act. The result of which had been something in the nature of a prose passage.

Initially, various students had come up with random statements capturing what had happened; thus:

I walked into the classroom, holding a piece of chalk in my right hand. Standing in front of the students, who were eight in number, I then greeted them. They responded to my greeting. After that, I wrote the statement "I walked into the classroom" on the board.

What had ensued was much in the nature of what Chi had predicted. About the very act of my walking into the classroom, we had gone into animated debate. Some of the students had been of the opinion that, in that act of walking in, I had appeared overtly nervous. Others thought that I had indeed been nervous, but not so nervous as to suit the implications of "overtly". Others still thought I had appeared courageous, although quite uncertain about what to do next. Others still thought . . .

The contributions had sprung up in abundance, like mushrooms rising up in sequence. In the communal search for the exact word, the class had become so worked up that all inhibition seemed to have vacated our otherwise quite reserved natures – as though, in fact, an invisible bottle of wine were circulating among us. And it had taken us a whole two hours to transform that initial passage into:

With some measure of assertiveness and a fleeting touch of fear, I trod into the classroom, a piece of chalk peeping from the clutched fingers of my right hand. Facing the students, yet to some extent avoiding their glances, I said "hello" to them in a voice tainted with an elusive tremor. The students, numbering ten but studded all over the room, responded in a tone not entirely shorn of the element of disbelief. Thereafter, I turned around hurriedly, and, in a handwriting that also underscored a tremor, wrote, on the board, the statement "I walked into the classroom".

Poetry had proved even more enthralling. Beginning with the statement *This room is hot*, we had, here too, tried to work out the details. As I had learnt long ago, Poetry, ever more so, is about matching feelings with words. That, in fact, the most original poetry was the feeling itself. That in the very hiss of a ravine – therein lies the poetry. That in the very glare of sunshine – therein lies the poetry. That in the very touch of the loved one, in the very fragrance of the acacia – therein lies the poetry. That, in short, words are but an attempt to imitate sensation, or to tap into nature – and that, as such, even the best written poetry can only be an approximation.

In spite of this, or, perhaps, because of it, that imitation is far from being an easy task. And so, we went through another heated session, the students and I, trying to find the words which, as much as possible, conveyed the intended meaning with more fidelity than *This room is hot*. We ended up with

We're tilting two storeys
Above the ground's embers.
But the embers have spread
Their prongs of molten lead;
And even in our loftiness,
We're gripped in the blaze
Of thick walls of concrete –
Panting and gasping
In the stiffness and stillness
Of this chamber of fire.

I must admit I found the sessions quite engaging myself. And while having consciously sought to provoke unbridled thought, I would find myself caught up emotionally. In the sweep of it all, I would find myself giving vent to feelings which I had never once thought lay within me. In the engulfing lure of self-expression, I would find myself saying things which, later, I couldn't always puzzle out.

Not that every idea of mine found favour with the students. No. The students would point out how such and such a view of mine failed to convey the intended meaning. If it spelt a contradiction, they said it did. If it oozed with understatement, or screeched with overstatement, they said it did. From time to time, some would brand such and such a contribution of mine as "sheer absurdity" – or "absolute nonsense".

Then, frankly, I would feel rather overstretched – vexed, in fact, at being thus corrected by the very people I was supposed to correct. But I would try to remind myself that the aim of the whole exercise was to discover the truth, as much as was possible under the circumstances. And in the quest for truth, no matter how unattainable truth is, there cannot be half-measures.

I was about to clock one full month in the job, I think, when the Head of my Department burst into one of my classes.

"I think you're going too far," he panted, tumbling over his words.

The classroom was full; so full that some of the students were sitting two-to-a-chair. But now, at Dr Ndinendekha's words, there was total silence. So much so that the beeping of a digital watch could be heard somewhere among the students.

"Going too far where?" I blurted, with a slight constriction in my throat.

"Look, mister," he continued, standing on the threshold, "I don't care who else comes to your classes, all right? But by all means, leave my students alone!"

"Which students of yours?" said I.

But at that very moment, a female student emerged from the gathering, and headed for the exit. "You see!" shouted Dr

Ndinendekha, spreading his arms across the doorway. "I always prove what I allege. Always!"

There then erupted a startling outburst from among the students. An outburst of strident whistles, booing and jeering. And there, in the doorway, Dr Ndinendekha looked on in sheer silence. His mouth agape, his lips hanging loosely, he surveyed the student gathering as if to ask, "Really?" Yet, he said nothing of that sort. Instead, he cupped his palms, then brought them together in a deep-toned clap, turned around and took exit. The female student in question, who had, in the meantime, been standing next to him, now waved to the class, then trailed after him – like a wayward daughter in the process of being rescued.

"We're tired of these people!" said one student, raising his voice above the general murmur.

"All right, all right," I said. "For your assignment, try to develop that line into a full-length argument."

"Which line?" several students asked in unison.

"The line: *We're tired of these people*," said I.

A thunderous bout of laughter reverberated in the room, bringing people out in the corridors to a standstill.

NINE

The following morning, I found a note in my pigeon-hole, at the University's reception (or Porter's Lodge), summoning me to appear before the Principal.

A bespectacled man in his fifties, the Principal was one for whom, I must concede, I did have a certain amount of admiration. As a student, I had had a few rough dealings with him. Like, for instance, in the aftermath of a punch-up involving police and students, and in which I had had a hand. But even in his punishment of me, I thought I could discern the actions of a man not entirely beyond reason. And now I realise that in some of those spiky dealings with him, we had been decidedly in the wrong. I realise, also, that the man would have been far more accessible to reason if it were not for what his blood-links with the country's ruling family demanded of him.

And now I was knocking at the secretary's door, wondering at the turn things were already taking. I had run into Vivi and Jah in the passage outside. Without asking the purpose of my presence there or explaining what they were doing in so unexpected a place, Vivi had said, "Don't give in!" and stomped off. With a look of disapproval, Jah had followed him.

I examined the sign in front of me – a sign which I had examined scores of times before, in my student days. It read: DR DZIKONDANGA – PRINCIPAL.

The secretary responded, and I went in.

"The Principal is still on the line," she said to me.

"All right," I answered, lowering myself on the rotating armchair. "Give us a beer, will you, honey?" I pointed at the giant refrigerator looming behind her.

"No. A cup of tea, Mr Unenesyo?" she asked, laughing.

I had had a little beer overnight, and at the mention of tea, I could feel my tummy churning. "No, thanks, madam!" I exclaimed. "I'm under strict medical orders to avoid tea entirely."

She threw her neck backwards with laughter, remarking, "Mr Unenesyo! You haven't changed, have you?"

"Oh, I've changed a lot, madam. See? Now I'm growing a beard! Plus I'm wearing a tie!" I went on, brandishing my tie.

As she laughed again, the Principal appeared in the connecting doorway, and said, "Mr Unenesyo?"

"Hello. Good morning," said I.

"Come on in," he invited, indicating the way into his office with his palm.

I walked past him and into his office.

It was one spacious office, furnished and stocked so generously as to make my office cubicle, up in Room P look like some stone-age, mobile latrine.

"Take a seat, take a seat," urged the Principal, indicating a seat in front of the coffee-table.

"Thanks," I said, sitting down. And, to my surprise, he sat down in front of me, across the coffee-table.

"Right!" he began, lighting a cigarette. "So how are you coping, Mati?"

The shift to the first-name basis went some way to boost my morale.

"Quite well, I'd say!" I said, almost tempted to tell the whole story.

"Really?" he probed, looking at me fixedly from above the rims of his thick lenses.

"Oh yes! The students are so motivated that one actually looks forward to the classes!"

He shifted in his seat, and knocked off ash into an ashtray placed on the coffee-table. "Unhuh," he grunted, drawing on his cigarette. Then, clearing his throat, he launched into: "I have information to the effect that you are stealing other lecturers' students. Am I rightly informed?"

I stared at the coffee-table vacantly.

"Well . . . I don't know if one could call it 'stealing', even in a figurative sense. I would . . ."

"OK, OK. Let's call it 'luring', all right?"

"Even 'luring' wouldn't do, Mr Principal. I just conduct my

classes as well as I can – like everybody else, I suppose. The students, of course, come of their own accord."

He maintained his silence, taking repeated puffs from his cigarette. "I see your point. I see your point," he observed, looking fixedly at some point on the carpet. "You will realise, nevertheless, that this University, like any other university in the world, runs on a set of established rules – not so, Mati?"

"I . . ."

"I mean, you've gone through the same system, have you not?"

"I have, yah," said I, as he squashed out his cigarette.

"And about the rules?"

"Oh yes, of course. Every institution runs on a set of rules, or something such."

"Something such?" he snapped, raising his bust to the upright position.

"I mean the rules, of course."

He looked at me ever more fixedly, his fingers dovetailed across his lap. "Er . . ." he resumed, looking about the coffee-table. Then, suddenly: "Do you realise that you're in a tight corner, Mr Unenesyo?"

"Tight corner?"

"Of course! I mean, you've obviously broken some rules here, have you not?"

"Like what?"

"Like what? Are you serious?"

"I mean, I don't know what rules I've broken!"

He gazed at me.

"Honestly!" I added.

"Oh, come on. You ought to know better than that, heh?"

I, in turn, just gazed at him, wanting to smile, yet unable to smile. Subsequently, his glance caught mine. And so there we were, just gazing at each other, as though we were considering whether to resort to punches or not.

"OK, look at it this way," he resumed, ending the spell of the glance, and clearing his throat. "To begin with, word has it that you teach without notes. Now, at this stage, I do not want to go into the details, such as pertaining to who might have imparted that idea to you."

"That's all right."

"What's all right – teaching without notes?" he yapped, looking up sharply. "Are you saying, Mr Unenesyo, that it's all right to teach without notes?" He stressed every word of it, the orbs of his eyes remarkably magnified.

"Well, the students end up with notes, as far as I know. You might want to look at the notes of the students in question, might you not, Mr Principal?"

"Me, look at the students' notes? Are you . . . Do you know who you're talking to?"

"Well, how else can you judge the contents of my lectures?"

"Look, I'm not interested in the contents of your lectures, do you hear me? I'm interested in whether you prepare notes or not; do you follow?"

"I see . . . I see . . ." I said, sitting up. "So as long as I use notes, you will be all right, is that it?"

"What do you mean – I will be all right? I'm not sick, am I?"

"I mean, any kind of notes will do, irrespective of their quality – is that the rule?"

"Heh!" he yelled, banging his fist on the coffee-table. "I don't care who is feeding ideas into you, do you get it?"

He looked me straight in the eyes, and I returned the glance in similar manner.

"Oh dear me!" he railed, slapping his thighs with either palm. "Do you want me to bring your Head of Department here?"

"Surely – if that will help illuminate the matter."

"What?"

I repeated what I had just said, wondering, for my part, exactly what it was he was getting so worked up about. Meanwhile, he was gazing at me as though I was the chap who threw a pearl into the sea, or the fellow that sought to commit suicide on his wedding day.

Then, breathing loudly, he rose up, went over to the connecting door, and said to his secretary, "Call Dr Ndinendekha, will you?"

Outside, the atmosphere was darkening. A rain-storm was determinedly in the making. My glance settled momentarily on the wall-clock: it was heading for nine o'clock. And I realised then that I was going to miss my fourth-year class, the most argumentative of them all. With that realisation, my spirits sank considerably, and I began to fear that it might affect my handling of this inherently unedifying matter. All the while, the Principal paced up and down his office, went over to his habitual seat behind the vast table, sat down, scratched his hair, and ended up lighting another cigarette. A moment later, he had risen to his feet and planted himself at the window on the extreme left. There he remained for a long while, examining the sulking landscape outside, absorbing the veering temperament of the unpredictable elements.

Some five minutes later, Dr Ndinendekha was ushered in. He was panting, but struggling to suppress it.

"I'm sorry to bother you, Doctor," the Principal began, lowering himself into the administrative seat. "Do take a seat, please!" He indicated one of the chairs in front of his desk.

I left the seat by the coffee-table, and went to sit next to Dr Ndinendekha – both of us thus facing the Principal.

"We have a problem here," the Principal pushed ahead. "Apparently, your colleague here," he gestured towards me, "is an adherent of the no-notes method!"

"Oh really?" exclaimed Dr Ndinendekha, looking at the Principal.

"Maybe you should ask *him*," said the Principal, drawing on his cigarette.

"Strictly speaking, gentlemen, it's not a no-notes method," I said.

"Nheh? What does he mean?" asked Dr Ndinendekha.

"As I was telling the Principal," I went on, "the students do end up with notes, after all."

"Who is talking about the students' notes?" asked Dr Ndinendekha, still addressing the Principal.

"That's the whole point!" cued in the Principal. "We're talking of the lecturer's notes, not the students' notes. You mean you're incapable of grasping that difference, Mr Unenesyo?"

"But what difference does it make," said I, my heartbeat going into high gear, "that I should have notes or not, if, at the end of it all, the students have notes?"

"What difference does it make?" the Principal yelled, again stressing every one of those words.

In that brief moment, I thought he looked unrecognisably different. Outside, a bolt of lightning zapped the air – so vividly, so viciously, that you would have sworn it had sunk into the earth. Several tense seconds elapsed, before a shattering explosion of thunder rocked the land to its very foundations.

"Oh, congratulations, Mr Unenesyo," the Principal said. "I forgot you are a Professor!" he added, laughing, as the rumble of thunder subsided.

"U-ha-ha-haaa!" Dr Ndinendekha laughed. "What! The fellow doesn't even have a Master's Degree! Ha ha ha! I mean, at best, he's only a student, isn't he? Yet he thinks he can teach without notes!"

There was silence. The kind of silence which, in gangster-movies, comes between the last words, and the moment when the guns are drawn. Suddenly, outside, the rains broke loose, and within moments, the drops were sputtering as though they had been doing so for hours already.

"Is it possible for you to take a look at the students' notes?" I asked, facing Dr Ndinendekha.

For the first time ever, he turned to face me. "You can bet I will!" he blurted, and then turned to the Principal. "It's part of my duty, is it not?"

"That will be kind of you," I remarked, rising to my feet.

"Wait! Who said you could go?" the Principal snapped, looking at me vacantly.

"Oh!" I exclaimed, sitting down again.

"All right," said the Principal, adjusting his tie. "Let us put it this way: Doctor, have a look at a few samples of the notes in question, then report back to me."

"I shall do that, sir," said Dr Ndinendekha. "But meanwhile, he must come to class with notes. I mean, rules are rules – no question about that."

"I think that's a fair deal. Wouldn't you say so, Mati?" asked the Principal, rearranging his pens in the rotating pen holder.

"In the context, I suppose so," said I, rising to my feet again.

I was about to start pacing away when the Principal suddenly launched: "One other thing, Mr Unenesyo. These gatherings of students that you are drawing are undesirable, to put it mildly. I need hardly remind you of the political overtones of such a phenomenon."

"I told you, I don't invite the students, do I now?" I snapped.

"Well, unfortunately, you'll be the one to bear the blunt – sorry, the brunt – in the long run!"

"For teaching Creative Writing?" I asked.

"No. For encouraging gatherings. I assume you know that this country does not tolerate gatherings, mister!" He ended with a short laugh.

"Can I say one more thing, Mr Principal?" I asked, feeling suddenly tearful.

"Go ahead. You've said lots of things already!" The Principal said, reaching for his cigarettes.

"Sir, this is the one and only University in the country."

"So?"

"We're supposed to be the light of the nation, sir."

"Go, mister. You've said more than enough!" The Principal waved me away.

I walked out of the office as, outside, the rain continued swelling as though it would never end.

TEN

When I explained all this to Chi, up in my hotel room, he responded, "Now you're close to the centre, Mati."

"To the centre of what?" I asked.

"To the centre of what this University stands for."

I went over to the bathroom, to close more securely a tap that had been hissing.

"It's strange, is it not?" I resumed, upon my return, wiping my hands on a towel.

"Phenomenal, I think," said Chi, sipping his beer. "But actually it's very simple."

"Simple?"

"Yah. Simple."

I fell silent, distractedly fingering my glass of beer, which was positioned on the dressing-table. The glass of beer looked so real in the mirror that you could have reached out and tried to take it. "Well, when they've had a look at the students' notes, and if they think the notes are OK, maybe they'll change their minds about it all," I pursued.

"Ah, Mati!" Chi exclaimed, laughing.

"What?"

"You're farther from the centre than I gave you credit for."

"Really?"

"Hundreds of kilometres away, I'm afraid."

I looked at him for a while, lifted the receiver and ordered two more beers from the Hotel's bar. By this time, I had received my first salary. And, surely enough, the money was diminishing at the rate of water in a hole-riddled bucket. To this day I keep wondering how a man could teach in a university, only to earn less than what a cleaner earns in a country a little to the south.

Out in the passage, the clinking of glasses announced the imminent arrival of the waiter.

I settled the bill, and let the fellow go with a few odd coins.

To hear him utter his thanks, you would have thought I had just told him the secret to eternal life!

"What was that about my being hundreds of kilometres away, Chi?" I pursued, after having downed a generous amount of the beer.

"It's very simple, Mati," said Chi, lighting a cigarette. "If they think the notes are good, then you will truly be in the tight corner the Principal spoke of."

"How now?"

"It's the difference between Manthaland and most of the countries I've been to, Mati. In those countries, if you know how to chop firewood, they'll give you the sharpest axe, and piles and piles of firewood. In Manthaland, they'll take the same axe, and chop your head off – literally or otherwise."

There was silence. "And that is why," Chi went on, "even a billion years from now, we won't have been developing long enough to have become developed."

"But why, Chi?"

"Why what, Mati?"

"Why this distaste of the very people that could save Manthaland?"

"Well, you'll soon find out why, Mati. You've probably been recruited to decode just that law."

"Heh, Chi! Can't one decode anything on the side of happiness?"

"I'm afraid not, Mati. In happiness, we merely put into practice what we learn in sorrow. What women learn through the pain of child-bearing, for instance, we men are unlikely ever to know."

"My mother used to say so too."

"There you are! And I think that, precisely, is the symbolism of the Crucifixion."

I took several sips in succession, as though in a hurry to get somewhere. Then, I do not know why, I grabbed Chi's cigarette, which was busy smoking itself away in the ashtray. And though the first few puffs made me choke, in another few moments, I was smoking smoothly, as though of old.

"Well, don't take it out on yourself, Mati," Chi said with emphasis.

"I don't know, Chi," said I.

"Look, Mati, personally, I'm quite certain that if every talent on earth were allowed to come to the fore, everything would be invented in twenty-four hours. Everything, that is, save Life. You imagine what that could mean for mankind, Mati?"

"It could mean everything, I should think. But why can't Life be invented, Chi?"

"Because Life is that which causes the inventing. It is the Agent, do you see? You can invent something, but you cannot invent that which invents. To put it differently, you can invent a box, but you cannot invent yourself."

"I think I understand."

"Fine. But the point I was making is: don't be so hard on yourself. Because though one must always do what one can, it must always be remembered that things can only be one way at a time; never two ways at the same time. So that the best policy in life, if there ever has to be a policy, is to take everything easy!"

"That sounds like Oscar Wilde!"

"It *is* Oscar Wilde."

We laughed for a long time.

In the meanwhile, we had timed our leaving my hotel room to coincide with Kettie's knocking-off. And as we got into Chi's car, there she was, running up like a child, the stilettos resounding on the gravel, the strap of her handbag sliding off her shoulder every time she reset it.

"You sure knock off late, miss!" Chi said, as Kettie eased herself into the back seat.

"Oh n-o-o! This is only 8 p.m. There're times I work up to midnight!"

"It's one hell of a difficult job," I remarked, as Chi reversed the car.

"Yah!" Kettie sighed. "Those of us who are not smart enough – we always end up with jobs like that."

"No, Kettie," Chi said. "Nobody is smarter than another."

"Really?" asked Kettie.

"Yah! It's all a matter of concentration," Chi went on. "We spoke about concentration the other time, didn't we, Mati?"

"We surely did, Chi."

"Put a labourer in an environment where he can concentrate ninety per cent, and he'll discover the Law of Gravity as much as anyone else," Chi said, laughing.

As we rolled towards the Highway, I explained to Kettie, in her mother-tongue, what Gravity was all about.

"I mean, almost all the chaps who repair radios and watches in this country have never been to school – isn't it so?" Chi pursued.

"It is," said I.

"That's it!" Chi exclaimed. "Concentration. It's all a matter of concentration!"

"I'm glad to hear that, Chi!" said Kettie.

We all laughed.

As we rolled on the Highway towards Kogan, it began to feel as though my relationship with Kettie was one of those that turn out to be durable. But then every relationship, as long as it lasts, does exude the impression that it will last to the very end of existence. And perhaps in that lies the joy of it all. For the prospect of the end mars the very beginning, blurs the duration, and maybe hastens the end in itself.

ELEVEN

We arrived to find Chi's yard pulsating with life. The flames were leaping, the music was blaring. There was a hiss of roasting meat, there was a hum of voices – all part of the general bustle that had transformed the orchard into a living mass of motion.

By now, I was acquainted with most of the folk who crammed Chi's yard – people who, as Daisy had pointed out, always came to Chi's place as their whims dictated. And now, as we stepped out of the car, they welcomed us with whistles and ululation, handshakes and exchanges of greetings. It turned out that Kettie herself knew most of them, having lived and worked in Testingtime Hotel for quite some time. And although Daisy came from Lolagar, the bustling capital, and Kettie from the far-flung North, the two took to each other right from the start.

"Have you noticed, Mati," Chi was saying, "that women take to one another more readily than men do?"

"Oh yes, I have," I returned. "And maybe they're right who say the world would be a better place if we guys were not in it."

"Of course!" said Daisy, serving the wine. "Only, I would still go out there and fetch my Chi!"

"Where?" Chi asked, drinking.

"I don't care where," said Daisy. "Mars or Jupiter – it doesn't matter!"

We all laughed.

As on previous occasions, the garden was glowing with the golden hue shed by the fires of the barbecue. But also, high up in a cloudless sky, the moon smiled its boundless smile; its diffuse, milky fluorescence scattered about the orchard with surreal enchantment. Though it had rained drenches only that morning, the sun had long baked the land dry and crispy, and people were sitting on the grass. There was a music system outside in the orchard, with loud-speakers placed high up in the trees. And now, as Kettie and I went to sit on the terrace, the music came seeping soft and unhurried, like the mild twittering of the birds of dawn up in the woods of faraway Patichi.

"It's a little like a dream, over here," Kettie observed, as we sat down.

"Indeed – a dream come true." I edged so close to her that I could feel the warmth of her body and the arousing scent of her perfume.

"Here," she went on, lifting her wine-filled mug to my lips. "Drink a little of this."

I sipped sparingly. Then, in turn, I lifted my mug to her lips, saying, "Here, drink a little of this. Drink softly, for you drink of my dreams!"

She also sipped, her lips barely touching the edge of the mug. "What was that you said?" she then asked.

"About?"

"About dreams."

"Oh! I was using the words of an Irish poet."

"How do they go?"

"Tread softly, for you tread on my dreams," I recited, fiddling with her hair. I had a fleeting desire to recite Yeats' entire poem beginning "Had I the heaven's embroidered clothes", but I knew I couldn't recall it all.

"Those are touching words," sighed Kettie, kissing me briefly on the lips. "Do you also write poems, Mati?"

"Once in a while, yes."

"Really? Some day, you'll write a poem for me, won't you?"

"Maybe!" My mind then hooked onto something, and I added,

"*And when the time comes*
Maybe I shall write
Of the night we sat together
In a glowing garden –
Where the fire leapt softly

To the drone of mounting voices
And where music,
Like the distant notes
Of little shy birds,
Came floating gently –
Ever so gently –
Upon the soothing breeze
Of Lake McSilence."

"No-o-o-oh!" she exclaimed, patting me on the chest. "Where did you learn that?"

"From here," said I, kissing her on the lips swiftly.

"Aaaaah!" she guffawed. "What about me?"

I eased my mug, then her, onto the terrace. I then wrapped my arms around her, and, slowly, our lips sailed in silence towards the heat ahead. Sailed, met and locked – and everything went swirling, turning and rolling like in the boundless realm of deep-night dreams.

"So that's where you learnt the poetry?" she breathed, when we had disentangled.

"Exactly so, miss!" said I, feigning emphasis. She began shaking her shoulders in suppressed laughter.

Later, when we had downed the wine a bit and I lit a cigarette she observed, "I didn't know you smoke, Mati!"

"I didn't know either, until recently," I said.

She was carried off with laughter again.

And so the night rolled on – rolled on and on. At some stage Kettie moved off and I joined Chi. Refilling my mug, he said, "Maybe we can now get to the bottom of a little mystery that has been intriguing me."

"Mystery?" I said, my head swirling with drink.

"Yes sir. You haven't yet told me which position you hold regarding women."

"Very simple, Chi. I prefer the normal position!"

"No, you bugger," said Chi, laughing.

"I don't mean that!" I went on, trying to sound serious.

When the bemused look would not disappear from Chi's face, I said, "In brief, Chi, I never . . . I never . . ."

"You mean you never go for them unless they go for you?"

"Not quite, Chi. Unless I think they have a similar inclination towards me!"

"Oh get off; you can't be serious!"

"I'm serious, Chi!"

He reached for his cigarettes, lying on the lawn, slotted out two, and we both lit up.

On the arena, the dancing was waxing hot as the folk tossed themselves about with varying degrees of frenzy. Farther across, beneath a mango tree, Daisy and Kettie were in an animated conversation.

"But now, how can you know they have some inclination for you, Mati?" Chi pursued.

"Murder will out, Chi – as they say," said I, relighting my cigarette. "Besides, it seems to me that telepathy is one of those things we call extraordinary, when in fact it is an everyday occurrence."

"Right, I concur with you there," said Chi, refilling my mug. "I mean, basically, we almost always know what the other person thinks. And where we do not know, we ask."

"That's it. Without that, people would always be colliding on the sidewalks, for instance, and boxing bouts would never last more than a second."

"Quite so, quite so. But I mean, Mati, what's the point, in this case?"

"With regard to women?"

"Yep!"

"Well, I find that it works better if there is some unsolicited mutual liking from the start."

"I don't agree with you, I'm afraid."

"You don't, Chi?"

"I don't. I mean, a relationship is like a house. It has to have a foundation."

"Of course, Chi. But the more easily a foundation is laid, the better."

"Nope! The more easily a foundation is laid, the sooner the building collapses, Mati."

"I see. So you don't believe in love-at-first-sight?"

"Nor at second, nor at third. I think love-at-fourth-sight seems more likely to me."

I exploded with such laughter that I spilled wine over myself. And presently, Daisy and Kettie came running towards us, with Daisy saying, "What's the joke? Let's hear it too!"

"Nope," Chi interjected. "Not until you tell us what you've been saying about us, you two!"

"Who's been saying anything about you?" retorted Daisy, as she and Kettie sat down.

"You and Kettie," Chi cued in. "I mean, half of their time, women talk about men. The other half, they talk about what men talk about women."

The two women were ripped apart with laughter. "And what about men, Chi – what do they talk about?" Kettie asked.

"We're more tragic, I'm afraid," Chi went on. "If we're not talking about how to get a woman, we're talking about how to get rid of one."

Again, the women reeled with laughter, with Daisy also spilling wine on herself. Thereafter, Chi and Daisy went in for a dance.

"Let's go for a dance too," Kettie said to me.

"No, dear, I don't know how to dance!" said I.

"Really?"

"Yep. Besides, I tend to think that dancing is the vertical doing of things that ought to be done horizontally."

Again and again, Kettie shook with laughter. "You're being naughty, Mati!" she enthused, still laughing. "You and Chi are both naughty. Very naughty!"

"Well, that's what you get when you cross-breed an English drunk and a Manthalandan drunk," I joked.

"I can almost believe that!" said Kettie, throwing her legs over mine. "But are you like that in class too?"

I emitted a short laugh. For the first time in hours, the issue surrounding the students returned to my mind. I thought of Dr Ndinendekha. I thought of the Principal – and all the scenes of that morning, in the latter's office, reeled before my eyes in gripping vividness.

I had to shake my head several times to dispel the vision. On the arena, Daisy and Chi were wriggling themselves about to the beat of the music, whose volume had now been raised to rather unsettling levels. The other revellers too were not to be outdone. Throwing their arms in the air, aside, or all around, they spun themselves about to the gurgle of both music and alcohol.

Decidedly, Chi was right, and Oscar Wilde before him: the secret of life was never ever to take anything seriously. For no matter how seriously or unseriously you took things, what has happened will always have happened. Events were ahead of one, in other words – always ahead even as they happened to one – while creating the sensation that one was inside them.

"You didn't answer my question, Mati!"

"About how we are in class? Oh well, I'll tell you some other time, Kettie. You know, there is a type of dance that needs no lessons."

"Is there?"

"Of course. Only, it's a horizontal type of dance, mostly!"

"There you go again. When is our marriage, by the way?"

"The unofficial one takes place tonight!"

"I see. With Chi and Daisy as the chief witnesses, no?"

"No, madam. With the bed alone as chief witness."

Again, Kettie went gurgling with childlike laughter, as, somewhere in the neighbourhood, the yapping of dogs rose above the music.

"Enough of the dancing," Chi panted, as he and Daisy now threw themselves next to us. "Daisy, go fetch some more wine!"

"Wine or swine?" Daisy snapped, as she went up the terrace towards the house, leaving us rolling in an outburst of laughter.

We ate and drank, smoked and talked – until I-don't-know-what dreadfully odd hour of the night.

I woke up the following morning not knowing where I was. This time, however, I was certain it wasn't Testingtime Hotel. And then?

And then, who was this other person sleeping by my side?

Why – Kettie, of course!

We were on a wooden bed in none other than Chi's house, in the sitting-room, what's more! I remembered then, as though from another world, that Chi had talked of a bed and a mattress lying in the store-room. I remembered, also, that he had lit a second, or a third, hurricane-lamp. But as to who had brought the bed and the mattress to the sitting-room, that I couldn't remember. And, from then on, there was but a void – like the nagging void left by all dreams which rub themselves out as soon as one awakens.

"Heh, did the marriage take place?" I whispered into Kettie's ear.

"Yah," said she, drowsily. "About half a million times."

We started laughing, our voices grown husky, and quite unrecognisable. And, laughing, we drew our heads under the blankets yet again . . .

TWELVE

I went to class on Monday still without notes. Chi's argument on the matter was quite simple, and, for me, wholly convincing: if one taught with prepared notes, and achieved the desired results, all was well. Similarly, if one could teach without prepared notes, and achieve the desired results, all was well, too. And matters of convention, to use Chi's own words, "had no role whatsoever in matters of knowledge".

To the fourth-year students, I began by apologising for having missed Friday's class. When they demanded to know what was going on, I told them that it had something to do with a slight misunderstanding, which was bound to clear up.

"Don't give in to fools!" one student shouted.

"Idiots!" another one hollered. "This is a university, not a reformatory, or any other form of penal institution!"

"Wait, wait, wait," I said. "I understand your feelings, ladies and gentlemen. But I hope you realise that what they are waiting for is some such outburst of sentiment from the students. And then, equipped with the benefit of false justification, they will pounce on us all in ways not difficult to imagine. Let us not, therefore, provide them with a motive. Let us simply do what we think is right – and, as you know, it is impossible to err on the side of right. Do you see what I mean?"

"All right," began one student. "But how can we achieve anything without doing anything? I mean, it's your kind of thinking that has brought this country onto its knees, is it not?"

"No, no, no, no!" another intervened. "We're not politicians, guys. We're academics, and as such . . ."

"What trash!" shouted the first student. "What does it matter whether we're academics or paramedics, heh? I mean, our lives are governed by politics, are they not? And, besides, we live in a country where a torn shoe is a political issue!"

A thunderous peal of laughter broke out, with some students shouting, "Prove it! Prove it!"

"You want me to prove it?" railed the first student. "Fine. You wear a torn shoe. The authorities interpret it as meaning you're poor. If you're poor, it has to be that the economy of the country is not working well. And if that's what your shoe is saying, you, the wearer, are saying exactly the same: you're criticising the government, by which simple fact you've dived head-first into the politics of sedition."

Again, a wave of laughter broke forth, bringing people to a standstill out there in the corridors.

Across the quadrangle, in Room Z, Chi was also busy conducting a class. His was packed so much that some students sat atop the desks – packed, indeed, as it had always been down through the years. And as our classes reeled themselves out, a messenger from the Administration Block knocked on the door of my classroom and handed me a note. It read:

Mr Unenesyo, come to the Principal's office
as soon as you finish reading this note.
DR M. DZIKONDANGA – PRINCIPAL

I looked at the students, my mind gone blank.

"We'll stick with you!" one of the students yelled, banging his fist on the desk.

"OK . . . OK!" I said, stuffing the note into my shirt-pocket. "When is our next class?"

"Tomorrow at three," several of them answered, all at the same time.

"Until tomorrow, then," I said, as I walked out of the room.

Somewhere along the corridor, a group of lecturers had assembled. Jah, too. He stood half apart, looking distinctly uncomfortable. As I went past, one of them said: "Heh, Mati, those shoes you're wearing, they can't have cost more than two pence, can they?"

"Not at all, sir," said I. "They cost as much as yours – which is to say nothing at all!"

"What about your hair?" another of them added. "When was the last time you shaved it?"

"The same year that you shaved your armpits!" I said, moving away.

"Wait, wait!" said yet another. "We understand you're going out with a receptionist. Is that accurate?"

"No, it's not. I'm going out with your wife!" I blurted, getting out of earshot.

So much for taking things easy!

Again, as I went past the Porter's Lodge, a Lecturer in Mathematics asked, "Do you know what a Junior Lecturer is, Mr Unenesyo?"

"Yes, I do," I replied. "He's a Maths Lecturer who accepts a labourer's salary!"

By that time, my fourth-year students had caught up with me, and, right there at the Porter's Lodge, they unleashed a roar of laughter that turned the heads of people in the corridors. Farther down the corridor that led to the Administration Block, I met up with Chi himself. Unknown to me, he too had been summoned to appear before the Principal.

"Are we such outrageous culprits, Mati?" Chi asked, as we went along.

"Far more outrageous than our mothers ever told us," I said, laughing.

"Fine; but you remember the rule, don't you, Mati?"

"I remember the rule, Chi – take it easy."

"That's it. Take it easy!"

"Still, I do think it would be wonderful to break a couple of jaws, all while taking it easy."

"No, Mati. Do you know what fighting is?"

"Yah. It's when you punch someone so fast they don't see it coming!"

"No, Mati. It is a sign that the intellectual faculties have failed entirely!"

I found myself laughing in spite of myself.

"Seriously, Mati," Chi persisted, even as we went up the steps leading to the Principal's office. "I mean, what's the use of having been to school, if, at the end of it all, you use your blows just like anybody else?"

"All right, Chi, all right," I said, adjusting my tie.

The secretary's door was wide open, and when we appeared, she told us to proceed to the Principal's office straight away.

"I don't know what to say, gentlemen," began the Principal, once we were seated in his office. "But as you will no doubt admit, something somewhere is going the wrong way." He stopped short, removed his jacket and hung it over the back of his chair. "Now what do you say to that, Prof?"

Chi lit a cigarette, rose up, went over to the coffee-table, and collected an ashtray which he positioned on the vast desk.

Outside, beneath the Principal's office and the library, lecturers' cars kept coming and going. And I thought of how truly beautiful it was to be teaching in this place. If you didn't have a class, you sneaked out and went where you wanted.

"Er . . ." Chi began, blowing a jet of smoke across the table. "I shall assume, Dr Dzikondanga, that we're talking to one another as academics. Would that be right?"

"Well . . . to some extent, yes," said the Principal, balancing his head, then lighting a cigarette, in turn. I also lit one.

"To some extent?" Chi pursued.

"Indeed! You will remember, Prof, that there are times I have to act purely as an administrator."

"A-ha!" Chi exclaimed, knocking cigarette-ash into the ashtray. "And I think that's exactly when tragedy occurs in Administration, Mr Principal – when Administration is divorced from the benefits of the intellectual faculties!"

The Principal remained silent, his glance riveted somewhere between me and Chi. "Let me put the Vice-Chancellor on the line, if you don't mind," he eventually said.

"By all means!" Chi agreed, laughing briefly.

As the Principal reached for the telephone, Chi's hand and mine met over the ashtray, and we flicked the ash concurrently. "That's called 'coincidence of wills'," said Chi, lowering his voice only towards the end. "People meet only thanks to the fact that their wills have concurred to do so."

"Not entirely, Chi," said I. "What if you bump into someone by accident, for instance?"

"You're not familiar with Freud, are you?" said Chi.

"The subconscious?"

"Yep. It makes us do things without our knowing why we do so, or, at times, even that we do so."

"Hello! Give me the Vice-Chancellor, please," the Principal's voice rang out.

"Even in dreams," Chi continued, "people meet only because they've desired to meet."

"But do we really meet in dreams, Chi? I mean, are the happenings of dreams real?"

"Why not, Mati? I mean, we see them, don't we? Why should they be less real than air, for instance, which we can't see?"

"Mr Vice-Chancellor? Oh, the Principal, here. I have Professor Chiselwood right here in my office. He would like to talk to you."

"Put him on the line, please," said a hissing, yet audible voice.

As the Principal pushed the cradle across the table, and handed the receiver to Chi, I pictured the Vice-Chancellor's office right up there next to the Parliament Buildings. Compared to that office, the Principal's office was but a scrap-yard waiting to be modernised. There, everything . . .

"Hello!" Chi began, crashing his cigarette into the ashtray. "Listen, Don. There're all sorts of things being said about academic matters here."

". . . aware . . . situation," the voice said.

"There's need for a meeting, I think. A . . . A . . . A meeting of all academic as well as administrative members of staff, as a forum where . . ."

"I'm thinking . . . that too," the voice hissed, becoming fainter.

"As soon as possible, yes," Chi went on, nodding his head. "Don, academic ethics are at stake here. You understand?"

". . . . ."

"Indeed! Imagine such a thing, Don!"

". . . . ."

"Fri . . . Friday should be fine. OK . . . OK!"

". . . . ."

"It's a duty, isn't it?"

". . . . ."

My attention, meanwhile, had settled on the Presidential portrait, which was hanging on the wall that the Principal was facing.

That is how it was: in every office, the Presidential portrait hung on the wall in the direction that the office-occupant faced. Not only that, it had to hang, always, at a higher level than any other picture in the office. Any contravention of those rules was deemed an insult to the President, and led straight to jail.

Beneath the portrait, the names and academic qualifications of the President lay splashed out in their immutable order: His Utmost Excellency Dr Kham Kham: Eternal President of the Republic of Manthaland; Creator and Founder of the Blessed Nation; Chancellor of the University of Fearfong; Dismantler and Embalmer of Colonialism; Saviour of the people and the animals of Manthaland; Owner and Purveyor of Land, Wind and Water; PH.D, M.D., F.L.S., G.B.G, B.L.M.R., B.A., B.ED., LL.B., D.D., X.X.K.H.U., G.G.Y.V.

"They're only students, of course," Chi carried on. "They want to know, Don; they're hungry for knowledge. Does . . . Does that constitute a crime? Is that?"

Dr Kham Kham! For two-and-a-half decades, he had kept the Nation "on its knees", as the other student had put it. Kept it there and gagged and blindfolded it, exactly like a hostage. And sitting here, in this my exile, I wonder if things really could have changed much. It is now a year since Dr Kham Kham was eventually replaced. But then in Manthaland, institutions rarely die, if they ever die at all. The names, certainly, change just as easily as clouds change their patterns. But even taking things at their most optimistic level, I can well picture loans both foreign and local still being swept under the carpet with much pomp and glamour. I can well picture the regional divisions getting deeper and deeper, while getting less apparent. The North receiving the crumbs, and being thankful; the South taking the cream, and still claiming more. And where there was a dust-road thirty years ago, there will be a dust-road thirty years later; where there was an insult reserved for a particular region thirty years ago, there will be an insult reserved for that region thirty years later – things which, by nature, eventually require the silence of many in the crowd.

"Friday, Don. Right . . . Right . . . Bye."

It was over. The conversation was over.

As Chi replaced the receiver onto the cradle, a stray wagtail popped in through one of the open windows, fluttered helplessly about the office and ended up perching on top of the Presidential portrait. Then, as if it had come to its senses, it took off and vanished through a different window, leaving a fluff of feathers floating about the office.

"The wagtail feeds on latrine-worms," Chi observed, addressing no one in particular. Then, shaking off the reverie, he said, "Oh, as you may have heard, the Vice-Chancellor is convening a meeting of both academic and administrative members of staff, scheduled for Friday."

"I shall liaise with the Vice-Chancellor, thanks," said the Principal, rising.

As we walked out of the Principal's office, I had a feeling verging on the desire to fly. To take not just to the skies, but much farther beyond, straight into outer space and there to feel what it is like not to live under Gravity: this Law which, in Manthaland, it seems, was heavier than elsewhere. To fly, yes! Like that stray wagtail which, though worm-bound, could fly to liberty.

At the foot of the staircase, we found Vivi, leaning against a pillar – just waiting.

"Heh, Mati," he began, "look where this pacifism nonsense of yours is taking you!"

"Look, Vivi, we can talk about that elsewhere, don't you think?"

"That's the point, Mati!" Vivi exclaimed, punching the pillar softly. "You've developed into a sissy, Mati. You really have. In your student days, you were a man. Now, you've turned into an intellectual mummy's baby. And look what's happening to you! Me, if a guy steps on my toes, I break his knees for him, and that's it!"

"Oh, oh, oh, oh," Chi laughed, "that sounds like the Law of the Jungle, mister!"

"Listen, Chi," Vivi said, gesticulating vigorously. "You got us appointed, right? Well, now it's our turn to show what we're worth!"

"By breaking people's knees, Vivi?" Chi went on.

"Their knees or their skulls – I wouldn't care which!" Vivi railed.

"Oh come on, Vivi!" said Chi, pacing away. "Go sleep it off, young man. It's most likely a hangover. We'll talk it over at the Hotel, OK?"

"Fine, if that's how you see it!" said Vivi, laughing. "I'm in Room 25, Block C."

"No, let's meet in the Hotel's bar, all right? How is eight o' clock for both of you?"

"Eight o'clock is fine," said Vivi, laughing, shaking his head, and heading towards the Law Department.

"And for you, Mati?" Chi continued, as we went up the corridor leading to the Porter's Lodge.

"Yah, eight o'clock is fine," said I.

At the Porter's Lodge, groups of students – Chi's and mine in the main – were walking about, something like a mob awaiting news of survivors. And here and there, at safe distances, lecturers stood watching this unprecedented gathering.

Indeed, in a country where the very mention of the word "opposition" amounted to treason, who wouldn't have marvelled at a gathering of this sort? In a land where the very mention of the word "democracy" had led many to solitary confinement, or even to the gallows, who wouldn't have been stunned at signs of dissent? In a country where "Yes" was the only mode of survival, who wouldn't have shuddered at the mushrooming of a "No"?

Yet, Chi's intentions, as far as I could read them, were hardly ever geared towards an upheaval – not, at any rate, an upheaval of the political kind. His, as he had told me, was a revolution of the heart, that very root from which everything sprung. And if this whole thing was going to lead to disaster, I thought, it would be because we, no less than the authorities, had read something else into Chi's intentions.

As we walked into the student gathering, Chi said, "Ladies and gentlemen, all is well – if 'well' is the word to use. We resume classes tomorrow."

They broke into jubilation there and then – screaming, whistling, ululating, and trampling the pavement like in a stampede.

That evening, as I was passing by Jah's hotel-room, his door suddenly sprung open, jolting me slightly. "Hi!" he said.

"Oh Jah!" I exclaimed. "How is it going?"

"Step on in," he said, stepping aside. His eyes had taken on a hard, dark colouring and I knew he had been smoking "the other stuff", as the student-expression had it. I stepped in anyway. Jah closed the door behind me, and when he proceeded to lock it and to put the key in his pocket, I became certain that something sinister was in the making here.

I sat on the dressing-table, facing him.

"So you're busy kicking up a lot of noise on Campus, ain't you?" he began, pacing up and down the room, snapping his fingers.

"Well . . . If that's how you want to put it," I said, my heart doing an I-don't-know-what strange dance. "Otherwise, I just conduct my classes as well as I can – like everybody else, I suppose."

He looked at me briefly, emitted a short, dry laugh and proceeded to do the splits directly in front of me.

"You know what?" he declared, springing upright again. "Me, I can tear you apart into mincemeat in a matter of seconds."

"Mincemeat?" said I. "You're planning to set up a butchery, are you?"

"Don't play smart with me!" he snapped, stopping for a moment. "You probably don't know that I'm into karate, do you?"

"Karate?" said I, shifting about slightly. "That's the name of an Italian car, isn't it?"

He began backing towards the door casually, laughing beneath his breath. In the next second, he had projected himself into the air head-first, and was sailing towards me like an incensed bull.

Then, at the very last moment, I shifted an inch – just an inch – off target.

Hooop!

He crashed against the mirror in a din that must have been heard blocks away. The mirror instantly disintegrated into a myriad shards, some landing on the table, others flying off in all directions.

I had slid away, and was now standing next to the door. For some moments, Jah stood stooped in the position in which he had butted the mirror. It was as though he were trying to determine whether what had happened was an earthquake or a volcano, and how come, in particular, he was still standing there. Then, slowly, he lifted both hands to his head – and, discovering that it was still in one piece, he straightened up gradually, till he stood upright. Having done so, he turned hesitantly, until he was facing me.

"I fucked up the mirror, Mati!" he gasped, his lips agape.

"You sure did! You know what the French say? *On fait rien qu'à soi-même.*"

"Meaning?"

"Meaning: Whatever you do, you do it to yourself."

"Yes, but what are we to do, Mati? That's fifty bucks off me, man!"

Then, from out in the passage came the resounding din of approaching boots followed by a flurry of violent, enervating knocks. And, before either of us could answer, the door handle was being twisted about frantically, followed by yet more knocks. It was the watchman.

"What's happened in here?" he blurted, once Jah had opened up. Soon enough, he noticed the debris, and his glance shifted straight on to the board that was supposed to be the mirror.

"Oh, er . . . a mouse!" Jah mumbled. "A mouse slithered over my feet. Me, I thought it was a snake, and in the panic of it all – the mirror broke!"

The old man merely combed his glance up and down the room. "That's rather strange, you know," he finally said, as Jah lit himself a cigarette. "I never knew we had any mice in this Hotel."

"I saw the mouse myself," I mumbled in turn.

"Oh really?" The watchman turned to face me.

"Heh, Papa!" Jah snapped. "If two lecturers say there was a mouse in here, then there was a mouse in here. Do you hear?"

In Manthaland, a Lecturer is a person who, despite his thin pay packet, earns enough in one month to pay a watchman for the rest of his life – pension included.

"Oh, I'm sorry, I really am sorry," the old man now mumbled, retreating out of the room. "I shall . . . I shall tell them to come and clear the debris."

He vanished there and then.

"Shake my hand," Jah said, extending his hand to me.

I shook his hand.

"It's just that I think your association with Chiselwood can only lead to tragedy, Mati," Jah added.

"It may well be," said I. "But for me, as for many other people, Manthaland is itself a tragedy."

Jah merely spread his arms apart.

Later, in my room, as I readied myself for my appointment with Chi and Vivi, I had a series of sudden impulses to retreat on this whole thing. But I soon remembered that a guy has to take it easy – either that, or he goes to hell by the shortest route possible.

THIRTEEN

I dropped in at the reception just as it was approaching eight. "Listen, Kettie," I began. "What would happen if I smuggled you into my room one of these nights?"

"Very simple, Mati," she said. "I'd get fired."

"You're not serious!"

"I am serious, Mati. It's in the rules."

I remained silent for a while, then said, "Oh well, there're so many fire-extinguishers around, are there not? If they fire you, I'll put the fire out!"

"It's no joking matter, Mati," she sighed, paging through a batch of forms. "You . . . You like to joke even about serious things."

"Yah, but I mean, I may be in the hotel for months to come, you know."

"Months?

"Weeks, or months. It all depends on how soon, or how late, they find permanent accommodation for one."

"We'll be married by that time, I suppose – won't we, Mati?"

"Maybe. Assuming we don't divorce before then, Kettie!"

As she laughed, Vivi walked in, and said, "Chi hasn't come yet, has he?"

"No, Vivi," I replied. "But he'll be here soon."

"Gee, I'm dying for a beer, Mati. You'll find me in the bar, when he comes!"

"In the bar!" Kettie exclaimed, laughing. "Why are you guys always drinking?"

"That's for your husband to answer, not me," Vivi retorted, walking out.

Later, when Chi had arrived, and we had settled in the bar, Vivi said, "Me, my dad is Chairman of the National Airline. But I won't stick to decorum, or whatever else they call it, down on Campus."

"The point is not about decorum, Vivi!" Chi retorted, even as one lecturer after another walked into the bar.

"What is it about then, Chi?" Vivi pursued, drinking.

"It's about being nice, Vivi. Do you know a French writer called Chateaubriand?"

"Writers!" Vivi laughed. "I don't care for writers, Chi. They recommend lots of things that they never do themselves. I mean, they talk like idealists, but live like everybody else."

"Chateaubriand," Chi continued, "Chateaubriand says, whoever has a gift – and everybody has a gift – must use it in service to his fellow men. If he lets the gift waste away, he is punished first with a kind of personal malaise, and then, sooner or later, the heavens unleash some dreadful punishment upon him. I'm not quoting him word-for-word, but you see what he's getting at, don't you, Vivi?"

"Word-for-word or not, to me it makes no difference, Chi. I mean, what, for instance, did the guy you're quoting do for the French?"

"His *writings*, Vivi," said Chi, lighting a cigarette.

"Writings! How many people read anybody's writings, Chi? Or even those who read, how many act according to the things they read?"

"It all depends on how much concentration they read them with, Vivi. Shelley once said: Poets are the unrecognised legislators of society."

"Ah, lots of twaddle, I tell you!" Vivi laughed. "I mean, while poets are busy legislating, politicians and priests are busy re-legislating against poets, as well as against everybody else!"

"I think he has a point, Chi," I said, swallowing my drink.

"Fine, but is the poet to start breaking people's bones, just because politicians and priests are legislating against him?"

"Well, it so happens that I'm not a poet, Chi," Vivi replied, "nor do I intend ever becoming one!"

"But you're a lawyer, Vivi. I mean, you depend on words as much as a poet does, don't you?"

"Good!" exclaimed Vivi. "But wherever words don't work, I use my fists. And that's it, Chi."

"But where would we be if everybody used their fists, Vivi?" Chi pressed on, even as Vivi called for another round of beer.

"Well, where is Manthaland now, without ever having used any fists, Chi?" Vivi shot back.

"Oh my goodness. What do you say, Mati?" Chi turned to me. But at that very point, the Mathematics Lecturer walked into the bar, the fellow who had said something about Junior Lecturers that same morning.

"There is Professor Chiselwood and his acolytes!" the Maths man now shouted, above the music and the hum of voices. Now Vivi was a chap with bulging chest muscles; so bulging that if his shirt was unbuttoned, as was the case now, you had the impression that he carried pumpkins where he ought only to be carrying nipples. His biceps, to be sure, were bulbous enough to serve as speed bumps. On the whole, this was a man whose very handshake could have given you rheumatism, if not outright shock!

And now, as soon as the Maths chap had finished speaking, Vivi shot to his feet, trudged towards the counter, grabbed him by the biceps, and dragged him out of the bar as if he weighed no more than a kilogram!

"If I see you in this bar again, forget about your teeth!" we heard Vivi shouting from outside.

And indeed, the Mathematics fellow never returned to the bar: neither that day, nor any other day that I can recall.

"You see!" Vivi enthused, as he returned to where Chi and I were sitting, and as many lecturers left the bar without even finishing their drinks. "It works better than any volume of poetry I've ever read!"

"Vivi, Vivi," Chi said, shaking his head. "I thought the purpose of education was to train people how to use their minds, rather than their hands."

"Well, me, I use both, Chi!" Vivi retorted, as people looked at us in sheer silence. "I mean, I'm not a writer, or whatever, to be saying plenty things but never doing anything about them. I believe that the only possible fight is a fist-fight; the rest is politics."

"Ah. Ah!" Chi gasped. "What do *you* say, Mati?"

"Well," said I, "the point about the system legislating against poets seems valid to me. I mean, if governments were run by what poets generally say, I doubt there would be a single instance of injustice anywhere on earth."

"Keep talking, Mati!" Vivi encouraged me, drinking.

"But the point about all writers engaging in lip-service, and the point about fists: those two need to be looked at more carefully, I think." With that I lit a cigarette.

"I didn't say *all* writers, Mati!" Vivi protested, also lighting a cigarette.

"OK, if that's the case, fine. Because, I mean, you and I are here thanks to Chi – and Chi is a writer."

"OK, Mati. I wouldn't possibly be ungrateful to Chi, would I? Move on to the point about fists. You can't conceivably say anything against that, can you, Mati? I mean, as a student, you did a good deal of fist-fighting yourself, did you not?"

"I did, Vivi. But I think most of it was ridiculous."

"Ridiculous? Why did you do it then?"

"Why did I do it? Well, look, Vivi, from time to time, we do or say things we eventually regret."

"That's it, Vivi." Chi gestured to the barman to bring another round of drinks. Then he continued, "I mean, isn't life, in fact, about trying to do a little better, all the time?"

"Wait, Chi!" Vivi shouted. "You said 'most' of the fighting was ridiculous, Mati. Didn't you?"

"I did."

"All right. That means you think some of it was justified, not so?"

"I'm afraid so, Vivi."

"Mati!" Chi exclaimed, his eyes widening.

"Wait a moment, Chi," I blurted. "I think where fists are the only option, then I guess they're the only option."

"Nonsense, Mati," Chi protested, drinking. "Violence is violence, and nothing can excuse it."

"Not at all, Chi! In Law, we have what we call fight in self-defence, don't we?"

"All right," Chi agreed. "But in what defence were you acting just now, Vivi, when you threw out the Maths Lecturer?"

"In defence of my honour, sir. My honour and Mati's."

"Really? Does 'self-defence' include defence of one's honour?"

"But wait a moment, Chi!" I jumped in. "'Self-defence' does include defending oneself in circumstances where one's life is in danger, does it not?"

"It does."

"Well, isn't that a case in which violence is excusable?"

"OK. Let me put it this way," Chi sliced the air with his palms, vertically. "The Law, of course, is full of flaws, and the 'self-defence' clause is one of the flaws, I think."

We went on discoursing and drinking; smoking and arguing. In all that time, Vivi kept insisting that, as far as he was concerned, words were for times of peace, and that beyond that, one either fought, or one became a politician!

Towards midnight, we hit the town at large. But as to what happened there, my memory is quite misty; and about all I can claim to remember is that Chi made out two cheques to the value of £500 each – one for Vivi, and one for me; that, in a different bar, Vivi told a bunch of undercover cops to go to hell, and there burn to ashes; that, finally, Vivi went ahead and grabbed himself a lady-of-the-night.

FOURTEEN

The following morning, painted in red across the main bulletin-board on Campus, were the words:

CHI, VIVI AND MATI.
ALL ELSE TO HELL.

The work of students, in all likelihood.

I sailed through the corridors, reached my cubicle, and dialled Chi's home-number. "Chi," I puffed, "they've got our names in graffiti across the bulletin-board!"

"Really? Which bulletin-board?"

"The one at the Porter's Lodge."

"Oh shit! They're about to bungle the whole thing."

"Exactly what I thought."

Chi was silent for some time. "Oh well," he finally said, "what has happened, has happened. Not so?"

I was silent for some time too. "Well, I guess so," I managed to say.

"Good. Just go about your usual business. I shall be along in a little while."

"OK. I'll try to establish contact with Vivi too."

"No, don't, Mati!"

"No?"

"No. He'll just be too full of fire after last night."

We both laughed, then hung up.

They had, as I'd feared, definitely read something else into Chi's intentions, these students. Yet, again, the fact remained that what had happened had happened, as Chi had underlined. So the best course of action was to take things easy.

I was about to go to my nine o'clock class when Vivi stormed into Room P. Of all the new recruits, Vivi was the only one whose office was not a cubicle in Room P. Of all of us, only he had managed to find himself an office all of his own, down in the Law Department. Just how he had achieved that, I had yet to find out. Perhaps it was because of his father, but I wouldn't be too surprised to hear that he had flexed his muscles in front of whoever was responsible for allocating offices, somewhere in the Administration Block.

"Did you see the stuff at the Porter's Lodge?" he panted, drawing on his cigarette.

"Heh, man, what's going to happen?" I wondered aloud.

"Anything, my friend. As long as there're no guns involved, I don't give a shit!"

"OK, look, let's see how it develops, all right? Meanwhile, I think all extremes are to be avoided, not so, Vivi?"

"There will be a plain-clothes cop in your class today, Mati."

"What are you talking about?"

"About a plain-clothes cop. In your class, and another in Chi's class."

"What? How do you know, Vivi?"

"Me? My dad is part of the system, as you know. So you could say I'm your ear."

I fell silent. And presently, Jah walked into the room, said hello, opened his cubicle, and quickly began dialling a number on the phone.

"Get to class, man!" Vivi urged me, preceding me out of the cubicle. As we went down the steps that led to the ground floor, he said, "If I were you, Mati, I would tell the cop to evacuate before I started the class. You saw how I told them off yesterday, didn't you?"

"Yah. But I think they know whose son you are. The rest of us cannot afford to . . ."

"Listen, Mati, if you're saying I'm part of the system, I'm gonna see real red before you realise it!" Vivi's lips were quivering.

"OK, OK, OK! Look, Vivi, I'll see you after class. I'll see you after class!"

We headed in opposite directions, for our different classes.

But, remembering that there would be a cop in Chi's class too, I turned back and caught up with Vivi. "I just thought I should remind you to phone Chi about who would be in his class today."

"OK," Vivi said, his lips still quivering, "come to my office for a moment, Mati."

"Are you angry, Vivi?" I asked as we went along. "Look, I didn't mean you're part of . . ."

"I said, *come to my office, Mati*!"

As soon as we had entered his office, Vivi said, "Look, Mati, you and I are friends, OK?"

"Of course, Vivi."

"Fine. But if you step on my toes, I'll forget all that and break your slender body for you!"

Again, my heart began doing that very strange dance, and I kcpt saying in my mind: Takc it casy, takc it casy! But prc-sently, I put my pieces of chalk on the table, and said, "Can I show you something, Vivi?"

"What?" he said, rolling up his sleeves.

"No, no. I'm not about to punch you or anything!" I stretched my arms in front of me. "Do you see these arms of mine?"

"Yep. So what?"

"If I concentrate my mind into them, I can make them stiff as steel and you'll never bring them together."

"OK. Try it!"

It was a trick I had learnt in my days as a herd boy, way back in Patichi when I spent long hours out on the open plains, passing the time by matching my strength to that of the other boys – and I now tried it again. Coming forward, Vivi wrapped both of his vast palms around my wrists, tightened his grip, and tried to bring my arms together. He had a grip strong enough to strangle an ox; but a trick learnt in youth is a trick learnt forever, and try as he could, Vivi never once managed to gct my arms together.

"OK, you win, old chap," he finally said, letting go of my wrists.

"So you see, Vivi," I began, breathing down. "I'm the last person to lecture you on violence, or against violence. But this physical force, on which you bank so much, and on which I used to bank not long ago, is just brute force that one musters in a moment. There is nothing inherently meritorious about it!"

"Rubbish, Mati. You know what I've discovered?"

"No."

"I've discovered that you and I can demolish a whole bunch of unarmed cops – and we'll do it one day!"

"Oh, Vivi!" I gasped, picking up my pieces of chalk. "I'll see you later." I walked out.

It was as Vivi had warned. In the ever-increasing mass of students, there was a face that did, indeed, look foreign to the Campus.

"Today," I began, addressing the class, "we'll try to concentrate on what is termed discursive writing."

I wrote *discursive writing* on the board.

"You see," I went on, "there does come a point at which, to achieve more immediacy, to make the feeling more directly accessible to the reader, you may feel compelled to go right into the mind of your character, rather than having to report the message to your intended reader."

The pens rolled on paper, including the pen of the alleged cop. "Thus," I proceeded, "instead of writing *He thought that life is beautiful*, you may merely put down the thought such as it might flow in the character's mind: *Life is beautiful*. Instead of writing *He thought, in addition, that at times, however, the beauty of life is elusive*, you might put down: *Yet, at times, that beauty is elusive*. And so on."

"Like drinking right at the brewery?" one student asked.

"Like drinking right at the brewery!" I conceded.

"And getting very pissed, too!" another student added.

A roar of laughter ensued.

"In other words," I continued, "you imagine that the words you're writing are the character's mind itself. And so, you try to follow the entire process of the character's thinking – all the stretches, all the meanders, all the drifts, on and on. You try to follow the character's flow of thought, in other words, a phenomenon technically known as 'interior monologue', or 'stream of consciousness'."

"Why 'monologue'?" another student asked. "The character is talking to someone within himself, not so?"

We debated that point, and came to the conclusion that, indeed, the whole process might better be termed "interior dialogue", or, less controversially, "stream of consciousness".

"I don't care what it's called!" yet another student shouted. "To me, it all sounds like cerebral autopsy."

There was another cascade of laughter. Out there, around the Porter's Lodge, the numbers of students were steadily on the increase.

"Now," I resumed, "let us take a subject like 'spying', and let us assume that our character has somehow arrived at that subject." I wrote *spying* on the board. "What do you imagine your character might think along those lines?" I asked.

At that very moment, the alleged cop packed up his pen and pad and silently slid out of the room.

"Who the heck is he?" one student asked.

"I reckon it's a cop," another said.

"Come on, let's follow him and have done with him!" still another shouted.

As the entire class rose to its feet, I shouted, "Wait, wait, wait! He hasn't done anything wrong, has he?"

"What do you mean, sir? The guy has been spying on us!"

"He came to listen, as far as I know. And anybody has the right to listen, not so?"

"Oh no, sir!" one of the students shouted. "This softie-softie stuff of yours will lead us nowhere!"

"Heh, guys," I interjected. "You seem to forget that the other chaps have got guns."

"And you, sir, you seem to forget that we've had enough of this shit!"

"OK, OK. Let us try to develop the passage on 'spying'," I said. "We'll see if there is a clue in it for us."

After much further bickering, we did get to working out a passage on "spying". The tempers thereafter did seem less volcanic, from which I concluded that whatever else writing may achieve, there is no doubt that it is a form of exorcism.

FIFTEEN

At the main bulletin-board, the graffiti had now been rubbed. In its stead, there was a notice that read:

THE VICE-CHANCELLOR WILL ADDRESS
THE ENTIRE STUDENT-BODY
TODAY AT 7.00 p.m. IN KHAM KHAM HALL

BY ORDER
THE PRINCIPAL

I resolved to return to my cubicle and phone up Chi in his office.

As I walked back along the corridor, the same group of staff emerged from around the corner, ahead this time, with the Mathematics Lecturer among them.

I turned into another corridor that lay between me and them, and took several detours to get to my cubicle. Chi's number was engaged. I dipped the hook and dialled my brother's number, back in Timatami. The last time I had spoken to him, he had told me that his wife was down with malaria.

"Hello, Krom? It's Mati here," I said on the phone.

"Heh, you know what, Mati?" My brother sounded excited. "I was about to lift the receiver to phone you, exactly at the moment you phoned!"

"Coincidence of wills, Krom. How is your wife?"

"Back on her feet. And how is our Kettie, and how's Chi?"

"Both doing fine. Look, Krom, the cupes are up and about, and it doesn't look too good."

"Cupes" was Krom's word for "cops".

"Keep clear of them, Mati! They cabled three chaps from our office only yesterday." That meant they arrested three of Krom's colleagues!

"OK, Krom, I'll try!"

After hanging up, I dialled Chi's number again, and got him.

"I phoned you ten minutes ago," said Chi, on the phone.

"I've just come out of class, Chi."

"And how did it go?"

"There was a guest – the unwelcome kind of guest!"

"I see. And how did you receive him?"

"We dealt with the concept of 'stream of consciousness'. We were about to explore the theme of 'spying' when our guest made off."

"Great! I'm told I'll be having a similar guest, too!"

"I gather so."

"Me, I'll explore the theme of low pay packets, as related to dreams!"

"Oh yah, Chi, I've been trying to puzzle out what you said about dreams, in the Principal's office. Have you got a moment to spare?"

"I'll be going to the next class, in some twenty minutes' time."

"Fine. Look, you were saying dreams are as real as anything else. Is that it?"

"Sure."

"Where do they take place?"

"In the mind, of course. Where else do things take place?"

"Yah, but I mean, they can, for instance, take you to all sorts of places, whereas, in reality, you're only in your bed."

"Indeed, but even in our waking hours, we can transport ourselves to anywhere – to America, to Asia, whatever – all while being in Manthaland, not so?"

"All right. But you wouldn't say you've been to America, or to Asia, just because your mind happens to have strayed to those places!"

"OK. Let me put it this way, Mati. If someone were dead, and they took his body to Russia, would we say that person whose body it is has been to Russia, on that basis alone?"

"No."

"Why?"

"For then the mind wouldn't have been there with him!"

"That's it. In the end, it's the mind that determines everything. The body is just contingent."

"It's what?"

"Contingent. An accessory. Just like an envelope to a letter."

I remained silent.

"Mati?"

"Yah, Chi!" The reciever had gathered sweat and I shifted it to my other hand. "Look, there is a particularly bothersome dream I had on the eve of my coming to Fearfong."

"You recounted the dream to me, in Kogan."

"Did I?"

"You did. On the very first day, during the barbecue."

"Ah, ah!"

"So it's like you think it will happen, is it?"

"Yah, Chi!"

"But it's happened already, Mati."

"Where?"

"In the dream, of course."

"Fine, Chi. But there're dreams that project into the future, are there not? Premonitions and stuff!"

"Even if it happens, it'll never happen exactly the way it happened in the dream. It'll be an incident in its own right. Rather, a mere tremor, or a ripple, of the first and original incident."

"You accept then that certain dreams bear reference to the future?"

"Mati, the future, the past, the present, are merely contingent."

"What do you mean?"

"They're the result of the body happening to be on a planet called Earth, which rotates and turns in relation to something called the Sun, and so gives the semblance of day and night, of winter and summer, and so on. There're no such things where there is no solar system – in outer space, as you might call it."

"You mean time is . . ."

"It's a mere physical factor, like being in a particular pub, or a particular forest – to which we have been conditioned by virtue of our being in this portion of the universe."

"I see."

"The body, in other words, has interiorised, biologically, the notions of day and night, winter and summer, and such like. The subconscious mind, unlike the body, is independent of all such factors. And dreams take place in the mind."

"And so?"

"And so, on the level of dreams, there is no present, future, or past, or winter, or summer, or autumn."

"But why then do certain dreams point to certain incidents in our waking life, even if the resemblance is only partial?"

"It's the ripple effect, Mati, or the tremor effect. When we sleep, we're at the level of the universal, as we've just been saying. A level where there is no time, in other words. And there, you can live – dream, if you will – an incident that, in the waking world, took place thousands of years ago. Or thousands of years from now, perhaps."

"I see. I see. But why the duplication, even if only partial?"

"It's the same incident, but viewed under the constraints of Earth – the shackles of Gravity, the optical distortions, day and night, and so on. You know that a drop of water on Earth does not behave the same way as a drop of water in outer space, don't you?"

"Sure. In space, it can float as a whole; on Earth, it splits."

"That's it. What we see in dreams is the whole. What we see on Earth are the distortions."

"I see, Chi. I see!"

"And that is why there is something called art. Art attempts to attain to that universal, that whole, which we've been speaking of. You've heard of Surrealism, haven't you?"

"Yah. André Breton and company?"

"Right. That's what they were about. Their art was concerned with the world of dreams. And even science is tending more and more towards that. It's leaving the localised province of earthly contingencies, and moving into the comprehensive, universal dimension. I'm talking of a kind of physics which tries to account for all physical phenomena in the universe, rather than all physical phenomena on Earth only. The kind of physics that Einstein threw himself into."

"You mean art should not evoke everyday, banal experiences?"

"It should evoke whatever it evokes, Mati. As long as through what it evokes, we can reach towards the universal. In the same way that sleep – a banal, everyday occurrence – helps us to attain the sublime realm of dreams. In the same way that a stream leads to the river, and the river to the sea."

"But can that sort of thing really be attained, in art?"

"One hundred per cent? No, I'm afraid not. But, as in everything desirable, one has to try it, and perish in the endeavour."

I remained silent.

"I have to go to class now. Can you come over here at about eleven?"

"Heh, I was about to forget, Chi. The Vice-Chancellor will address . . ."

"I know, Mati. Can you come here at about eleven?"

"OK."

"Fine. See you then."

As I sat there thinking, the phone rang and Evelyn, the secretary of our Department, said, "Will you please come over, if you can?"

I said I would.

The cubicles were now, for the most part, filled with their owners. And as I left my mine, the chap in History spoke, through the louvres, "Don't you think, Mr Unenesyo, that I should be the only Assistant-Lecturer occupying a cubicle?"

"Really? Why so?" said I, locking my cubicle.

"Because I specialise in Stone Age History!"

The laughter from everyone in their cubicles resonated as if from the very caves that the History chap was alluding to.

I met the secretary even as I was going up the steps to her office.

"You'll excuse me, Mr Unenesyo," she began, "but I just couldn't say this over the phone. Nor could I come to your office, where everybody hears what everybody else says."

"It's all right. What's happening?" I said.

"You're due to go overseas for your Master's Degree, are you not?"

"That's how it normally works."

"Fine. I received some forms yesterday afternoon from the United Nations office . . ."

"Which forms?"

"Scholarship forms for you. When I came back this morning, they had vanished."

"Really?"

"Seriously! From my drawers – someone must have pinched them."

A group of students was now walking down the corridor, towards us. I thought there was something funny about the way they clustered together as they went, but I paid no further attention to it.

"Who do you think stole the forms?" I said to the secretary.

"I have some idea who could have done it. But I don't want to lose my job, Mr Unenesyo. I mean, nobody has the keys to my drawers, except me and Dr Ndinendekha."

As that group of students drew level with us, I saw that the Mathematics Lecturer was among them, at the rear. Presently, as the students continued their way towards the residential area, the Maths chap halted and said, "By the way, when are you going abroad to upgrade your low status, Mr Unenesyo?"

"When they've promoted you to Vice-Chancellor, sir," said I.

As the secretary giggled, the Maths chap began moving on along the corridor, saying, "Very well, Mr Assistant Lecturer. And when will that be?"

"You'll let me know when, Mr Vice-Chancellor!"

Another group of students appeared from around the corner, and the Mathematics Lecturer promptly paced away.

"What . . . I thought he was from your part of the country?" the secretary now said, pointing in the direction of the Maths Lecturer.

"He is," I pulled up my shoulder and smiled at her. "But never mind. What were we saying?"

"The scholarship forms!"

"OK. Look, Evelyn, your job is on the line here, as you say."

"That's right. I suggest you go and phone the United Nations office first, Mr Unenesyo, then you can follow up the matter with Dr Ndinendekha."

As I walked back to my cubicle, I reckoned that while phoning the United Nations office would be an attempt not to compromise Evelyn's job, it would, at the same time, be a stab below the belt to Dr Ndinendekha – even if he never found out. With that reasoning, I turned around, and began pacing slowly towards Vivi's office.

SIXTEEN

Towards eleven, Vivi and I headed for Chi's office, where we found him seated at his desk, surrounded by dozens and dozens of sheets of paper scattered all over – even on the floor.

"This book of mine doesn't seem to be getting anywhere," he said, as we sat down. And so saying, he relinquished his pen, threw his arms skywards, gesturing sheer futility.

Day in and day out, whenever he was in his office, Chi laboured away on this "book" of his. At that time, all I knew was that it had something to do with Being. And although I was in Creative Writing, it never ceased to amaze me that someone could spend so much time on something that may never even become a book. Little did I know then that the same manuscript would end up in my hands. And sitting here, in this my exile, I dip my cup into it, and draw these droplets . . .

"That's the problem with you writers!" Vivi began. "You battle with words but are content to watch the world go to the dogs. I mean, when I say 'writers', I except you, Chi, plus any other writer who is into action."

"You've said those things before, Vivi," Chi retorted.

"I know I have, Chi. But I'll say them again. I mean, on the whole, when something goes wrong in a country, or in the world at large, the last people to stand up are the writers themselves. Just imagine that!"

"They stand up in their writings, Vivi," Chi argued. "Writings which stand up not only to one historical incident, but to all such incidents for now and for all time."

"Yes, but I repeat: who reads them, Chi? Look, it's all right for me, as a lawyer, to write some high-sounding paper on Jurisprudence, or that kind of stuff. It's all right! But, in addition, or more importantly, I've got to go out there physically, stand in court – and defend people from the arbitrary tentacles of state terrorism!"

"And if that fails?"

"And if that fails, Chi, I make an appointment with the Prosecutor, and slug it out with him – this time with fists!"

"But Vivi," I came in, "you're now an Assistant-Lecturer in this place, and not a defence lawyer in court."

"Fine! But that's only because my dad wanted it that way, believe me. And let me tell you this: once I've been abroad and returned with my Master's Degree, I'm out to the courts. As simple as that."

"That's all right, Vivi. But . . ."

"In addition," Vivi interrupted Chi. "In addition, while I'm here – in this disguised reformatory called University of Fearfong – I shall use words in the same measure as I shall use my fists. That Mathematics Lecturer, for instance, I'll sort him out before the week is over!"

"Vivi!" Chi and I said in unison.

"I mean it, guys! I've just been told that he has hired a number of students to sort me out, see? So me, I'm waiting for them, right? And if they don't come fast enough, I'll go to them pronto and bash their bones to splinters. Look!" Here, Vivi bared his biceps, and flexed them into lumps only slightly smaller than anthills.

"Well?" said Chi, turning to me.

"I can only say what I said yesterday, Chi," said I. "Where physical force is the only option, I suppose it's the only option!"

"Fine. But as intellectuals, we're here to find that other option, Mati."

"The non-existent option, Chi?"

"Leave him to his books, Mati!" said Vivi, unrolling his sleeves. "You and I will do it, when the time comes. I mean, the problem with most revolutionaries is that they end up embracing words. And so find themselves in the very politics they set out to fight!"

"OK, Vivi." Chi lit a cigarette with great deliberation. "The Vice-Chancellor will address the students this evening. If I may tell you, he was planning to, at that very address, to announce the dismissal of the six students who are regarded as the ring-leaders, and who are thought to have scribbled the graffiti that was discovered on the bulletin-board this morning. Now . . ."

"What are you getting at, Chi?" Vivi asked, lighting a cigarette too.

"What would you, Vivi, have done to prevent the dismissal of the said students?" Chi carried on.

"Well, let me ask first what you did yourself!"

"Me, I phoned Don hardly thirty minutes ago, and told him what consequences the dismissal was likely to have."

"And then?"

"And then he called it off," Chi answered. "But now . . . I'm not here to enumerate my good deeds; nor do I consider what I've just done as greater than what anyone else could have done. My point is, what would you yourself have done, Vivi?"

There was silence, in which one could hear the hum of the traffic outside, as well as the staccato of the typewriter in Chi's secretary's office.

"Well," Vivi began, "first, I must say thanks, Chi, for what you've just done, as for everything else you've accomplished in this reformatory. But me, if I had my way, I'd grab that Don of yours and drown him in a barrel of beer, if he is lucky, or dump him into Lake McSilence, if he is less lucky."

We laughed and laughed – until Chi's phone began ringing.

Now the man whom Chi called Don was, in full, Dr Donald Campbell, alias Vice-Chancellor. British like Chi himself, he had been with the University of Fearfong less long than Chi, and, on many major decisions, he had remembered to consult with Chi. I remembered him as the man who had saved me from being thrown out of university on the grounds of that punch-up in which many dental formulae were radically changed, including my own; a man who had once told Vivi, "You are a mad boy. But just don't try to be madder than this." Only, Donald Campbell was, more so than the Principal, directly answerable to His Utmost Excellency Dr Kham Kham. And that, one supposes, is where the balance went tilting.

That evening, with the Principal sitting on his right, and Mr

Koloboleta, the Registrar, sitting on his left, Donald Campbell was to be heard at his most official level.

"I did not want to address you prior to addressing the University staff on Friday," he began. "But the graffiti that appeared this morning, at the Porter's Lodge, has compelled me to do so. Now listen to this, all of you," he drank from a glass of water that had been sitting on the table in front of him. "Listen to this, and listen once and for all: if you have anything to do with graffiti, or any other misdemeanour, your days in this University are numbered. So numbered that they can be counted off the prongs of a fork!"

Sniggering and restless shuffling broke out among the students gathered in their thousands in Kham Kham Hall.

"Let me tell you this, to begin with," the Vice-Chancellor resumed. "Lots of you may not know it, but this is one of the few universities in Africa – if not *the* only university – where everything is free, including tuition. Not only that, we pay you an allowance, however meagre. Yet, in spite of all this, some of you want to turn around and indulge in subversion."

An awkward silence settled on the students.

"I repeat: your days are numbered!" The Vice-Chancellor sent his eyes from one side of the hall to the other. "We know who you are that are causing all this, and right now, consider yourselves as being merely on a stay of execution."

Nervous laughter unleashed itself.

"This is a final warning, let me tell you, the very final of all final warnings. You're here for education – free education, what's more – so stick to education. Avoid being led astray by certain maverick elements within or without Campus. For, believe me, when the time of the clamp-down comes, when the storm brewing up there decides to break loose, you'll be the first to bear the brunt. Those who have ears, let them hear!"

With that, he stooped down towards the Principal, and whispered something to him, and then to the Registrar. Amid almost audible resentment now emanating from the students, the Principal and the Registrar stood up beside the Vice-Chancellor, and the three of them headed for the exit.

SEVENTEEN

Still, the numbers of students didn't diminish – neither in Chi's classes, nor in mine.

As Friday approached, rumours began to circulate that a clamp-down on people who "gatecrashed" classes was imminent. Such a clamp-down, in fact, had been tried before on Chi's classes, over the years. But Chi had argued then that as classes were all free, no such rule made any sense at all – given that the right to knowledge was a fundamental birthright. Also, such a rule would have excluded plain-clothes police from dropping in occasionally, and so the move had petered out gradually. How the Principal intended to implement it now was a matter of pure speculation, to be ascertained, as most people saw it, on Friday.

And so Friday morning fell with a kind of crash on the University of Fearfong – a crash from which we would emerge either maimed or restored forever. By half-past-eight, everyone was seated in The Greatest Man Hall, which was to be found on the western fringes of Campus – by the road that led to Testingtime Hotel. And here, hundreds of lecturers and administrators sat in front of the stage, and dozens and dozens on the stage itself. In the front row of the stage was Dr Donald Campbell. On his right, Dr Dzikondanga, the Principal. On his left, Mr Koloboleta, the Registrar.

All was silent, save for the general hiss of coughs and whispers.

"Right!" began the Vice-Chancellor, rising to his feet. For some time, he struggled to adjust the microphone to suit his height. But each time, with an incongruous, ear-jarring screech, the microphone insisted on dropping to its previous position.

"One of those uncompromising gadgets," he remarked, leaving the microphone alone. "All right!" he resumed, amid the nervous laughter that ensued. "Ladies and gentlemen, with all of us gathered here as we now are, the entire machinery of our beloved University has ground to a halt. For that reason, I shall be very brief."

There was an outbreak of throat-clearing, during which the Vice-Chancellor drank some water. "Some of you may have some idea why we're gathered here today. Some of you may not. I shall be brief about it all, as I have just indicated . . . The fact is that something is going on on this Campus which cuts counter the grain of propriety. Completely counter!"

He again drank some water.

"As you may have heard, the main bulletin-board on this Campus was smudged with graffiti."

Again, he lifted his hand to the microphone – then quickly let go. "Unfortunately, those students responsible seem to have, or are known to have, some links with certain members of the academic staff."

The glances zoomed upon Chi, Vivi and me, seated as we were next to one another, beneath the stage.

"Now, without going into further detail, I wish to reiterate here what I conveyed to the students only three days ago. This University will not – and I repeat *will not* – brook any form of subversion from any quarters whatsoever. The lecturer-student relationship, as you know, is a very delicate one. It is a relationship that must be restricted to the classroom, and to the classroom only, where all social or political commentary is absolutely disrecommended – for want of a stronger word. Any breach of this rule can only have disastrous consequences – and about that, I need hardly be more explicit."

There was such silence that you would have sworn the hall had suddenly become empty.

"I am sure it is in nobody's interest to see this University plunged in the kind of chaos that plagues most foreign universities. Yet, if the present trend continues, a crisis is exactly what we're heading for. When I say 'heading', I mean heading 'head-first'!"

A gush of murmuring swept through the gathering, as Dr Campbell drank some more water.

"But – and this is a big 'but' – I know that as academics,

responsible academics, those concerned are capable of nipping the situation in the bud. It is, after all, in their own interest to do so."

The silence fell again.

"There is something else. This time something of a purely academic nature. I'm referring to those academics who lecture without notes."

Again, the glances converged on Chi, Vivi and me. "Now, although I cannot recommend the 'no notes' method, I may say that senior academics have the experience and know-how to use such a method. They have, after all, been using it all along. But all else must stick to the general rule, that of using prepared lecture notes. No notes – no class. I'm even tempted to say: no notes – no job! I hope to hear no further complaints in this regard. Thank you very much."

A thunderous applause dislodged itself. Some people remained seated, but others, still applauding, rose to their feet, and began leaving the hall.

"Excuse me!" Chi shouted, rising and making his way to the stage. Having reached it, he grabbed the microphone and, speaking into it, said, "Excuse me, I have something to say!"

"Yes, Professor Chiselwood?" the Vice-Chancellor shouted.

There was widespread murmuring, as those who had been standing returned to their seats.

"I said I have something to say!" Chi persisted, dragging the microphone aside, and adjusting it to his height. In his baggy trousers, his extra-large shirt, his shoulder-length hair, his thickly bearded chin, Chi might just as well have dropped through the roof, straight from planet Mars – particularly against the background of suits that adorned the stage.

"Certainly!" shouted the Vice-Chancellor. "As long as you remember to be brief, Prof!"

But Chi had already begun speaking.

"I wish to say something," he was saying, "partly in response to what the Vice-Chancellor has said, partly in response to my own conscience."

A wave of throat-clearing broke out again, with a corresponding shuffle of a myriad feet. And, for the first time, I noticed that scores of students were crowded in the corridor around the hall, the faces of those in the front row pressed hard against the louvres.

"To begin with," Chi said, adjusting the waist of his trousers, "I want to cast some light on what I consider as the role of an academic."

Again, Chi struggled to adjust his trousers.

"As I have often told my students," he continued, "being born is like crash-landing into a place where you can recognise neither anybody nor anything."

Laughter rang out, particularly from out in the corridor. "And all our lives amount to nothing more than an exploration of the strange surroundings into which we have been thrown. I have always felt that a child's cry at the moment of birth is a cry of anguish at the very gigantic mission which lies ahead of it."

Another bout of laughter.

"And so, with every glance it takes around it, with every touch it makes, with every faltering step it subsequently takes, the child explores the nature of the people and the things around it. And that exploration continues all the way through adolescence, through adulthood – right up to the moment of death."

"I wish you would come to the point, Prof!" the Vice-Chancellor called out.

"I am, Don," Chi said, stroking his beard. "It follows, from what I'm saying, that a person's mind is built up gradually from his exploration of the world. A man's mind really is only as wide as he has read, or as he has travelled."

"Come to the point, Prof!"

"I am, Don," said Chi. "And we, as academics, are on the forefront of that exploration I speak of. We have come a long way from that very first step of our toddling-days. But the distance we have covered is nothing compared to what we have yet to cover. The last words of Isaac Newton, if I can misquote him, went something like this: I do not know what I may seem to the world. But for my part, I've always felt like a little child playing on the beach, who amuses himself, from time to time, with finding a smoother pebble. And, all the while, the great vastness of the ocean's truth lay before me, wholly unexplored!"

"Prof!"

"I'm getting there, Don," said Chi. "There is no end to knowledge, ladies and gentlemen: for as soon as you've discovered the way to the moon, you discover also that the same way continues to Mars – and so on and so forth. In any field, be it Astronomy or Theology, be it Literature or Biology, or whatever, one way always leads to the next. And the role of an academic, of course, is to go beyond the point where everyone else stops. In short, ladies and gentlemen, knowledge is the reason for existence. The quest for knowledge, therefore, ought to be encouraged – indeed, facilitated – rather than impeded. And so, whereas a syllabus is such an expedient thing to the teacher, it must by no means be the end of our search."

From outside, the sound of applause invaded the hall, and was taken up by a few members of the academic staff – and amplified all over.

"It's all right to prescribe what should be taught," Chi went on. "But to prescribe, in the same breath, what should *not* be taught – that, ladies and gentlemen, amounts to nothing short of putting barriers in the path of knowledge. And let me ask you this, then: what kind of university are we, if we prevent access to knowledge? What kind of academics are we, if we stipulate boundaries to learning? This system by which the students cannot commune with lecturers, that amounts to putting barriers in the quest for knowledge. Because from everyone, from everything, we always stand to learn something new. This system of preventing certain books from coming into our libraries is the biggest insult ever to occur to intelligence. This system of preventing people, students and lecturers alike, from saying what they feel about the country, or about anything else – that, too, amounts to putting barriers in the search for knowledge."

There was silence.

"As for the so-called 'no notes' method, the controversy surrounding it is a result of sheer misconception. I have, frankly, nothing whatsoever against prepared notes. I myself, in fact, was moulded by teachers and lecturers most of whom used prepared notes. But I have since discovered that while notes may enable the student to pass examinations, the surest way to discovery is that of observation, and of individual thought. After material barriers, preconceptions are discovery's second greatest enemy. It is well to tell a baby how it feels like to walk, but until the child begins to walk, he knows not what walking is. More than that, the teaching he has received about it is likely to crash with his concept of walking, when he begins walking. I wonder if any of you have tried lifting something which you thought was heavy, but which, on lifting, turns out much lighter. The feeling of emptiness which one experiences in a case like that is what I'm referring to!"

The students unleashed murmurs of approval. Although he no longer interrupted Chi, the Principal could not keep his feet still.

"The search for knowledge is like climbing a tree. You climb it from the base, not from the branches. And however great it may be to know the Law of Gravity, for instance, it's far more helpful to mankind to contribute something oneself to the Law of Gravity. However admirable it may be to know the words of a song by heart, it does more service to mankind to go out there and sing.

"I need hardly remind you that some of the greatest discoveries on Earth were made often by sheer observation, or by sheer accident, so to speak. Newton did not discover gravity from reading volumes of books on physics. No. He discovered it from watching an apple fall. Archimedes, while taking a bath, discovered some law concerning liquids and solids which revolutionised the science of measurement. And history is full of such examples. What we witness today, in fact, is but the technological application of laws discovered long ago, in the most basic of circumstances.

"We're all brothers and sisters, ladies and gentlemen. Our various disciplines, as I've always said to my students, complement one another. They're all a probe, from various angles, into the mysteries of creation. They're all but a mere continuation of that first step we all took as toddlers.

"Ladies and gentlemen, let us go out there and continue the search. Only then can we be doing service to both our own journey and the journey begun by our forebears. Thank you very much!"

As though by prior agreement, the entire academic community stood up at once, followed by the administrators. The applause which ensued lasted for many, many minutes. Outside, the students whistled and screamed, clapped their hands and trampled the ground – all of which intensified as Chi came down from the stage, walked down the aisle, and out into the open.

EIGHTEEN

It was as though thick, dark clouds had cleared over Fearfong, and the sky was blue again. It was as though the dike of suppression had suddenly given way, allowing the floods of freedom to inundate the Campus. Kettie and my romantic strolls even took us up there, because just like that, the police had stopped coming onto the Campus. Just like that, the Students' Union, for so long a mere name, could now convene meetings on the issue of Human Rights. Just like that, the Students' Union could now openly question various aspects of the University's administrative system. On the catering front, in terms of health services, the lecturer-student relationship, things picked up so much that, sitting here, years later, I have some difficulty in believing that all that was happening then in Manthaland. And I certainly do recall that even to Chi himself, it was a phenomenon that had surpassed not just his expectations, but his intentions too. As the weeks spun by, even Vivi slowly came to admit that this was all right, describing it as an instance of the peaceful ruling over the peaceful.

But maybe he had precisely that to thank, in the matter of the threat from the Mathematics Lecturer. A week after Chi's speech, the Maths chap walked into Vivi's office, and said, "I don't think we have any more cause to 'slug it out', sir."

"As far as I can see, no," Vivi remarked. "Unless you're particularly keen on ending up in the mortuary, sir!" They both laughed long, and ended up shaking hands.

"You know what?" pursued the Maths chap. "There were some twenty students out there prepared to snuff the life out of you at the slightest indication from me!"

"Me?" Vivi exclaimed, laughing. "They must be mistaking me for a snuff-bottle, those boys of yours!"

They began laughing again.

It turned out to be the beginning of a deep-running friendship, a friendship which was representative of what was going on in the University at large. Not only was there more interaction between lecturers of the various departments, but students were now to be seen even in the Lecturers' Refreshment Room – talking to whomever they liked, and actually drinking!

It could be said, indeed, that it was the students who benefited most from these developments. Their diet had changed from "beans every day" to "beans never" as they themselves put it. The dismissal of female students on the grounds of pregnancy was declared unconstitutional – and so on.

With regard to Chi, Vivi and me, invitations to functions of various sorts were almost a daily occurrence. At such functions, Chi was invariably the guest-speaker, a task which he would, at times, delegate to either Vivi or me.

Nor were the students to be outdone, as far as invitations were concerned. On the slightest pretext, they invited Chi, Vivi and me to address them. And I remember, in particular, the laughter Vivi caused when, in a speech at a party, he once told the students, "What we're going through is what they call 'the golden age'. But I'm frankly quite puzzled how we got here without having to knock anybody's teeth out."

He had probably summed it up. Between me and Dr Ndinendekha, my Head of Department, not a single punch had ever been thrown. On the contrary, from time to time, we even went out together in his Mercedes Benz, drinking and arguing amicably. My scholarship forms had been found and sent off to Canada. It would be effective from the beginning of the year after. It was generally accepted that I would be successful, so until then, Dr Ndinendekha and I were to collaborate on an anthology of poetry.

My relationship with Kettie, too, was gliding on smoothly – although, on the issue of marriage, we never quite seemed to view things from the same angle. The authorities had, by now, found permanent accommodation for all the newly-recruited members of staff. Vivi had been given a whole house, located between the Testingtime Hotel and Campus. I, for my part, had been allocated a flat lower down along the road to Campus.

It was a cavern of some kind, that flat of mine, with the kitchen, the sitting-room, and the dining-room on the ground floor, the bedroom and the bathroom to be found upstairs.

"You've never really been clear on the issue of marriage, Mati," Kettie once said to me, during a weekend that she had come to spend with me.

"Marriage?" said I, reaching to the radio on the room-divider that separated sitting-room from dining-room, and turning up the volume.

"Marriage, yes!" said Kettie, sitting up on the sofa. "I've mentioned it to you twice recently, and, on both occasions, you have merely joked it away!"

"But isn't it enough that, as it is, we're happy with our love?"

"I'm not talking about love, Mati. I'm talking about marriage!"

"Oh, Kettie, they're the same thing, are they not?"

"No, they're not. Well, yes, they are. But love leads to marriage, and that's the difference!"

"Well, if it leads there, then it'll lead us there. I mean, why should we anticipate it, Kettie?"

"It doesn't happen on its own, Mati. It has to be talked about!"

I was sitting on a sofa, opposite her. And presently, I left my seat, and went to sit next to her. Then, looking into her eyes, I said, "Listen, madam, if we're in love, and love leads to marriage, then we'll get married without ever having rushed it."

"Oh, you mean we'll just wake up one day, and find ourselves married. Is that it?"

"No, we'll wake up one day, and find ourselves so much in love that we'll find ourselves standing in front of the District Commissioner."

"Why the District Commissioner?"

"He's the guy that marries people, is he not?"

"Oh Mati, Mati!" she said, laughing and patting me on the cheek. "It's the Magistrate who marries people."

"Well, that's who I mean, madam!"

"You educated guys are strange, I tell you," she observed, rising to her feet. "Take Chi, for instance." She went into the kitchen as she spoke.

"Bring me a beer, will you, Kettie?" I said, lying on the sofa, face upwards.

On the radio, they were playing *Walk of Life*, a Dire Straits tune which both Chi and I liked.

"For the past ten years, Daisy has been trying to get him to marry her but nothing has ever come of it!" Kettie emerged out of the kitchen with a beer and a bottle of wine in the one hand, and two glasses in the other.

"Well, that's the point, Kettie. You don't get anybody to marry you! It should happen as a consequence of love, if it is a consequence."

Kettie was about to say something when a car pulled up right into our front-yard. And who should get out of it but Vivi.

"Don't tell me that's your car, Vivi!" I said, as I opened the door of the flat and stepped outside.

"But I told you I was going to collect it, didn't I?" he replied, coming up the embankment.

"You told me?" I asked, as Kettie also emerged out of the flat.

"Ah, Mati, I told you my dad had bought me a car, and that I was going to collect it today from Scotland!"

"When did you tell me, Vivi?"

"Yesterday. In the Lecturers' Refreshment Room."

In the Lecturers' Refreshment Room yesterday, I had got myself sozzled beyond all description.

"He forgets everything when he is drunk," observed Kettie, standing next to Vivi.

"I know, madam," Vivi said, "but he didn't look drunk, then."

"Well, you guys drink without ever looking drunk, don't you?" Kettie remarked. "And this car of yours may soon become your hearse, unless you cut down on alcohol!"

"Oh well, one hearse is as good as another," said I, going down the embankment, and examining the car. "You got yourself a brand-new Mazda, Vivi!"

"It's from my dad!" said Vivi. "On my own, I'd never save enough money to buy a car. You know how long it takes me to drink the so-called salary that we're getting?"

"I have some idea, Vivi," I replied.

"Two days, to be exact! Look, give me a beer, will you? I'm dying of thirst; I drove straight from Scotland, non-stop."

As we entered my flat, Kettie said, "You've got a car, Vivi. What you need next is a woman. I mean, these ladies-of-the-night will lead you nowhere, will they?"

"She's got a point, Vivi!" I added from the kitchen, dislodging two beers from the fridge.

"What do you take me for – a sissy?" Vivi asked, taking the beer from me, removing the bottle-top with his teeth and proceeding to drink the beer straight from the bottle.

"What's a sissy?" asked Kettie, as we moved into the sitting-room.

"Anyone who indulges in softie-softie things – like love, non-violence, and such like."

"You can't live without love, can you, Vivi?" I asked, as we sat down.

"Well, I'm living, ain't I, Mati?" Vivi had already emptied his beer, and, presently, Kettie went into the kitchen and returned with another beer, which she gave to Vivi.

"It's an existence, Vivi, not a life!" Kettie observed, sitting next to me.

"Existence, or life, wind, or air – what difference does it make, Kettie?" Vivi said. "You cannot live two lives at the same time – and this is my life."

As we went on arguing, Hollywood Wonyada, my neighbour, walked in, saying, "So you guys are drinking without inviting me?"

"I didn't mean to get pissed, Holly," I said. "But suddenly, here is this Vivi chap in a brand-new car!"

"Which car – the one out there?"

"You guessed it!"

"He must have pinched it," Hollywood remarked.

"What?" blurted Vivi, sitting up.

"OK, OK, I'm just kidding," Hollywood mumbled.

Later, when all four of us were half-teetering with drink, Vivi said, "Let's pay Chi a surprise visit."

"Fine!" I exclaimed. "We go pick up some wine in town, and off we go!"

So off we went.

NINETEEN

The months roll on in this pleasant manner. December is a month away, and we'll soon be going to Patichi, Kettie and I. On Campus, all is going smoothly. I have been awarded the scholarship to Canada, and Vivi and I are due to leave for studies overseas, come January. We have celebrated this, Vivi, Kettie, Chi, Daisy and I. Our parents, too, have celebrated this, particularly my parents. Then, just like that, Daisy says to me, "Mati, Kettie sent me to tell you something."

"All right, go on," I say. We are at my place, Daisy, Chi and I. It is a Friday. Kettie is at work, and she is due to arrive in two hours' time, at about seven in the evening. The music is coming in softly and the wine seeping in slowly. I have not the slightest premonition of what is about to come.

"What, Daisy. What is it?" I ask.

Next to Daisy, opposite me, Chi is laughing beneath his breath. "She asked me to tell you not to get angry, Mati, and that . . ."

"Oh no, Daisy!" I exclaim, planting my glass of wine on the coffee-table.

"OK, OK," says Daisy, drinking. "She is pregnant."

"What? Who?"

On the radio, they're playing a Beatles tune, and it's going:

Yesterday!
All my troubles
seemed so far away . . .

"Kettie. She is into her second month," Daisy declares, refilling her glass.

I remain silent. I look at Daisy. I look at my glass of wine. I look at the radio. I look at the ceiling. Then I look at Chi, who merely says, "Remember the trick, Mati?"

"To hell with the trick, Chi. This girl is a crook!" I rise, and pace about the sitting-room.

"Fine, Chi!" I finally say, as I get back to my seat. "The trick is to take it easy, isn't it?"

"Exactly! Now get me a beer, Mati."

I go into the kitchen; I open the fridge; I pull out a beer for Chi. Daisy and me, we are on wine; and when that secretive woman called Kettie pitches up, she'll be on wine too.

Pregnant? How can she fall pregnant – she who told me she was on contraceptives, she whom, on some occasions, I actually saw swallowing the pill? How can she fall pregnant when I am about to go to Canada?

But then, a guy's got to take it easy . . .

When I return to the sitting-room, Daisy announces that she needs to go and see a friend in the neighbourhood. So she goes.

"You've known this all along, Chi, have you not?" I ask, as we continue swallowing our drink.

"For a couple of weeks, yah."

"And you never thought of telling me, Chi?"

"Well, Kettie didn't want anybody else to tell you but Daisy. And there is something called 'breach of trust', Mati."

"Fine, fine," I say, smoking. "What's a pregnancy in philosophical terms, Chi?"

"That's exactly the point which my book has reached!" Chi says, sitting up.

"Really?"

"Yah, I'm arguing, Mati, that conception and birth are spiritual concepts, before being biological. To begin with, there is a will which strives to take some physical form. And the sperm and the egg are merely the physical manifestations of that will. In the same way that flowers are a manifestation of love, or olive-branches a manifestation of peace."

"But where is this 'will', Chi, prior to its physical manifestation?"

"You remember we once established that everything we say or do presupposes a 'Yes'?"

"I remember vaguely. It was at the other downtown bar, wasn't it?"

"It was. The point is, you wouldn't do anything, even at gunpoint, unless you consented to doing so, however unwillingly."

"I remember."

"So there is a 'Yes' in everything. Even if you refused to say or to do something, there would still be a 'Yes' in favour of not saying or not doing that particular thing."

"I remember."

"Fine. That 'Yes' is the will. The question you're asking, then, is: where is that 'Yes' before it comes to us?"

"Where is it, then?"

"All over the universe. The universe is made of words, you know!"

"I don't see the link!"

"I, you, house, mountain, sky, Earth, Mars – all the way to universe – that's what makes it all. Without these words, including the words not yet in existence, there would be only one word: Nothing. But even 'Nothing' is a word, of course. Such that it is impossible to have a universe without words."

"Aaaah!" I exclaimed. "So the Bible is right, after all. In the beginning, the Word was with God; and God was the Word!"

"That's it; that's it!" Chi was smiling that same unbridled smile of his. "And if you read more, you'll find: 'And God said: Let there be light, and there was light.' In other words, it's due to God's mere mention of the word 'light' that there was light. It's God's willing that there be light which gave form to light. And that is why, at the human level too, you need only mention the word 'fire' for a whole army to start firing. The word equals the act."

I took several sips in silence. On the radio, they were reading the six o'clock news, of which the local items were about the tumultous welcome His Utmost Excellency Dr Kham Kham had just received in the Central part of the country; how people had braved pouring rains to see the Dismantler of Colonialism – and how these pouring rains were a sure sign of the bumper yield that could only follow.

"But now, the 'Yes' that leads to birth, who utters it?" I eventually asked.

"It drops out of the universal will, just like the word 'fire', upon which an army acts, drops out of the general's mouth."

"Yes, but in that case, there is an army-general to utter the word 'fire', is there not?"

"There is, indeed. And in birth, there is the owner of the birth, the one who is born, to utter the word 'Yes'. Have you noticed, for instance, that chicks actually peck their way out of the egg-shell?"

Indeed! As a child, I had observed that phenomenon scores of times. Sitting on my haunches next to Krom, I used to watch as he carefully lifted a broody yard hen with a stick to reveal some chickens crawling for cover and others still pecking at their shell-covering.

"In fact," Chi continued, "ask any mother, and she'll tell you that a baby emerges out of the womb partly through the mother's physical effort, partly through the physical effort of the baby itself."

"So I've been told!"

"The universe is a will, Mati. Which is why it cannot have any limits."

"It cannot have any limits?"

"No. A will has neither beginning, nor end. No limits whatsoever. Can you tell me, Mati, where your will to smoke cigarettes began?"

"At Testingtime Hotel, I suppose."

"At what particular moment?"

"The moment I picked up your cigarette, in my hotel room."

"And how short or how long is a moment?"

"Very short, Chi!"

"Yes, but how short is 'very short'? I mean, have you ever seen a slow-motion picture?"

"Yah."

"The same moment that it takes to make one step in everyday life can be made to last longer in slow motion."

"I see."
"And by speeding the film up, both the everyday step and the slow-motion step can be made to go faster."
"I see. So a moment is only as long or as short as it is perceived to be?" I filled in, going into the kitchen to collect more beer.
"That's it, Mati!" said Chi, as I put the beer before him. "A moment has no substance, except in terms of the action that is accomplished in that moment. In other words, 'time' is but a synonym for 'action'. And, depending on whether you like what you're doing or not, time can either be very short, or very long. Which is why, of course, one day in jail may feel like an entire week, or even longer."
"Right, right! I think somewhere, Shakespeare says: For in a minute there are many days."
"In *Romeo and Juliet*, yah! Have you ever had a dream in which you drop down a hole, or fall down a cliff and wake up instantly?"
"Several times."
"Good! Those are reproductions of how you once died – you and everyone else. And between that fall and the waking up, that's how long it takes between being born and passing on."
"Yes, go on."
"That's it, Mati. Life is but a moment spent in slow motion."
"I see."
"But to perceive it so is not a negation of life. It's just knowledge of it – just like the knowledge of microbes, or of outer space, or of anything else."
"Yes, I see. But let's go back to the will, Chi."
"Oh yah, the will is limitless, Mati. By the same fact, the universe is limitless, explainable only in terms of Creation."
"Really? What about the theory of the Big Bang, which has been proven?"
"That the universe came about following the explosion of a primordial atom?"
"Yah."
"It's simple, Mati. The Big Bang did occur, and all these

planets that circulate around the sun, for instance, are but the ripples which the sun made – and is still making – upon its exploding. But the explosion occurred only as a manifestation of the same will. How else could it have occurred, Mati? I mean, the fact that we know how a bomb exploded doesn't mean that the bomb must have planted itself, does it?"

"Not necessarily."

"Good. So we fall back on the will."

As I served myself some more wine, Chi said, "I'll go up to the toilet, Mati. This is a funny place you've got here, with the toilet upstairs." He started up the steps leading to the bedroom and the toilet.

"I'm considering moving out to a place like yours, Chi!"

"Not a bad idea. After the Master's, not so?" said he, stopping momentarily.

"After the Master's, yah."

I didn't want to think about the Master's because the Master's made me think of Canada and Canada made me think of Kettie being pregnant. So, while Chi was away, I went over to the kitchen, and returned with some apples.

"What you're saying," I resumed, as soon as Chi had returned, "seems to imply that everything in the universe has a will, not so?"

"That's what it means, yah!"

"So you mean rocks are living too?"

"Of course – why not?"

"Well, they don't have the same chemical composition as people or animals, do they?" I bit into an apple, like Chi.

"Mati, not too long ago, plants were thought to be non-living. Do you know that?"

"I do."

"And in any case, whether we call anything 'living' or 'non-living', they're still as much a manifestation of the will as the rest of the Universe. Whether we call air 'dead' or 'alive', it doesn't change the fact that the air is there, and that we wouldn't survive a moment without it. So, too, with rocks, which, upon disintegration, nourish plants and animals. So, too, with everything, Mati. It's . . . It's a whole ecosystem, utterly interdependent. Have you never wondered, for instance, why a volcano, which is but molten rock, erupts at one moment, and not at another?"

"The 'will', I suppose?"

"The will, indeed. If it chooses, a volcano can lie dormant for centuries on end. If it doesn't, it can erupt repeatedly over a relatively short span of time."

"And it's all a matter of will?"

"It's all a matter of will. Which, incidentally, explains why 'freedom' is such a big issue in the entire world. It has always been an issue, and will always be one. For the simple reason that freedom is synonymous with the will, and there is nothing that suppresses the will."

We drank in silence for some time.

"But what of death, Chi? Would that too be an act of the will?"

"Oh yes, that is said every day."

"Yes, but how is that?"

"Well, take a more ordinary occurrence, like drinking. All right?"

"All right!"

"In an hour or so, your will and mine will have tired of drinking, and they'll lead us on to some other activity."

"OK?"

"So there comes a time at which the will becomes tired of everything – of shifting from one activity to the other. It becomes, in short, tired of inhabiting the same body endlessly. It then vacates the body, and we call it 'death'."

"And where does it go then, or thereafter?"

"Well, that's like asking what happens to someone's desire to smoke, when they quit smoking. Or to a drop of water, when it drops into the sea."

"I see . . ."

"It's sucked into the general will, the universe, the everything. In society, the more strong-willed rule over the less strong-willed. And so the individual will, being of lesser magnitude than the universal will, can only be absorbed into the cosmos."

"And once it is absorbed?"

"Well, I suppose it's like a cloud hanging in the sky. The cloud is a whole. At the same time, it is made up of individual drops which, when they fall down to earth, we recognise as rain."

"You mean life is like a rain-cycle?"

"Like that, and like every other cycle."

"OK, the cloud comes back as raindrops. And us?"

"As anything!"

"As anything?"

"Yes. Trees, people . . . you name it."

"In that case, we're different from the rain-cycle, for instance."

"Why?"

"In the rain-cycle, the cloud always comes back as raindrops, and always as raindrops."

"Yes, but when the raindrops land on earth, they can land into anything, and take on the form of whatever they land in."

"Sure!"

"Us, too. We leave the parent will as multiple wills, and always as wills. But when we land, we land on anything, and take on the form of whatever we land in."

"I see. So where do heaven and hell fit in all this?"

"Have you ever woken up feeling particularly happy, or particularly unhappy?"

"Yah . . ."

"And have you noticed that the feeling continues through the day, at work or wherever?"

"Yah."

"Good. And have you noticed that if you sleep on a happy feeling, the feeling carries over into your sleep, such that your dreams are happy? And that equally, if you sleep on an unhappy feeling, the feeling spills over into your sleep, such that your dreams are unhappy?"

"Yah!"

"So, when you die, since your mind is still the same mind, exactly the same thing happens. If you die after a happy life, the feeling slides with you into the state of death, and it's called 'heaven'. Similarly, if you die after an unhappy life, the feeling slips with you into your state of death, and it's called 'hell'. Hence the importance of taking it easy!"

I drank in silence for long, long moments, went to the toilet, came back, and continued drinking in silence. When, a little later, Kettie arrived, about all I could say was, "Listen, Kettie, next time, try to tell me about it yourself – or consider yourself divorced!"

TWENTY

And then, as if that wasn't enough, Chi drove up to my place, the following day. "Don has just phoned me, Mati," he announced. "They are deporting him!"

"What?

"They're deporting the Vice-Chancellor, Mati. Within forty-eight hours."

"Ah, Chi!"

"True as true can be. He's got to be gone by Monday."

That was it! That was how it had always been! Throughout the decades since our much-acclaimed Independence back in the sixties, the pattern had scarcely varied. From time to time, along came a person who seemed determined to let even a minor breeze into the airtight chamber that was Manthaland. A breeze, that is, which would try to ease the economic asphyxiation of the wholly silent masses; to shake the bolts and wires of the political vice-grip of Kham Kham – and more than anything else, let the air flow again in several million souls. But people who had stood up thus, whenever and however, had faced one of two fates. If they were Manthalandans, they were fed to lions bred for the purpose. If they were foreigners, they were bundled out of the country within forty-eight hours. And slowly, so slowly, we had come to where we were – if we were anywhere at all. And sitting here, in this my exile, I realise we were caught up in a motion-without-motion – that very peculiar phenomenon I had noticed on the plane, on my trip of strange hopes into Fearfong itself.

And so, it had finally happened to Donald Campbell himself. I have to go back a little, and evoke what I indicated earlier concerning this man. That in his official capacity, Donald Campbell was much like Dzikondanga, the Principal: he said what he knew Kham Kham would want him to say, and that was it. In the meantime, however, Donald Campbell gleaned whatever information fell in his path, watched the situation blossom, and, on the basis of that, took a final decision.

By some such motion – for that, too, is motion – he had steered the University of Fearfong through almost a decade of otherwise total stagnation. He had passed where many before him had almost instantly found themselves on the next plane back to where they had come from. And maybe it must be said, not in deference to colonialism, but in deference to the truth, that without foreigners like Donald Campbell, the University of Fearfong would scarcely have arrived where it is today – if it is anywhere at all. Vivi, in any case, saw it this way too. I remember how, baring his lumps of biceps, he once said to me, "Call me colonial, or call me whatever else, but I think the tragedy of Manthalandans is that we lack completely the sense of public good!"

"What do you mean, Vivi?" I had then asked him.

"Simple," he said, laughing. "If, for instance, the money that went into the founding of this University had been entrusted to a Manthalandan, this University would never even have existed!"

That, I must suppose, sums up Manthaland. Not that we do not have the sense of justice. No. But for some reason which only money knows, the sense of justice which made us fight oppression in former times – that sense of justice quickly peters out once the tables have been turned and we have the reigns of power. It peters out, I say, and it does so quite invariably, quite implacably – and often as though by a non-divine determinism. It becomes, in short, the scramble for the National Cake; or, if we leave euphemisms alone, it becomes simply a case of who gets what and how much faster than whom, while the public, in the name of whom the powers that be had actually fought, watches with confusion, yawns with bemusement, and wallows about dreamly in a vapid aura of utter disbelief.

I've said it "peters out" – the celebrated revolutionary zeal. But I think that "peters out" is also a piteous euphemism. More particularly, that zeal spontaneously ceases to be; it evaporates like ether, thereby sublimating into the vague ionosphere of heated, mimed ideologies from which it must have dropped in erstwhile times. It thus comes as little wonder, if it comes as any wonder at all, that the history of Manthaland is of the briefest kind. We became Independent in order to become Dependent!

Maybe it's true what they say about stratagems and spoils: that those who fight are rarely the same as those who benefit. And maybe, also, Vivi had been right in saying the only possible fight is a fist-fight; the rest is politics. For sitting here, in this my exile, I cannot help but wonder how anyone can fight a system with full justification – and then, at the first opportunity, turn around and embrace the same system, with full justification, too!

But then, a guy's got to take it easy. Either that, or he goes to hell by the shortest route possible.

TWENTY-ONE

On Monday morning, all the students refused to go to class. Instead, they moved up and down the corridors in sizeable groups, up and down the lawns, shouting from time to time, "Where is Donald Campbell? We demand to know what's going on!"

It was only half-past-eight, but already, as we drove into Campus, Chi and I, the students were beginning to assemble at the main quadrangle, in front of the library. The lecturers, for their part, took one look at the set-up, and then either drove right back to the safety of their homes, or trotted off to their offices in absolute silence.

"I knew it wouldn't last long," Vivi remarked, as he got out of his car and joined us on the steps leading to the Porter's Lodge. "Nothing gold can stay!" he added, consciously or unconsciously quoting Robert Frost.

"OK, Vivi," said Chi. "Now just make sure you don't fan the sentiments of the students."

"Me? I'm going to tell them to go collect sticks, stones and steel pipes for when the cops arrive."

"Don't, Vivi!" I said.

"You're determined to see it come to the worst, aren't you?" Chi cued in.

"I don't care! If the cops come with force, we'll answer them with force!"

"And if they come with guns?" I asked.

"Then we'll bolt, of course!"

As we reached the Porter's Lodge, one student said, "This is it, gentlemen! You've done what you could, now it's the turn of us students."

"What's happening right now?" Chi asked, as more and more students congregated around us.

"Mba Nyi is going to address us all," a student explained.

"Addresses again!" Vivi exclaimed. "Just go and collect crowbars, do you hear me?"

"It's going towards that!" yapped another student, while Chi and I gazed at Vivi, speechless.

Mba Nyi was the chairman of the Students' Union – he who, indeed, had over the months led the students in their deliberations with the University authorities.

We all moved ahead, and joined the main body of students assembled in the quadrangle. And there, standing on the edge of the open corridor, Mba Nyi stood silently facing the students, a megaphone in his right hand.

"Right!" said Mba, speaking into the megaphone. "As you all know, ladies and gentlemen, the Vice-Chancellor is being deported even as I speak . . ."

"No ways . . .! No ways . . .! Hang them all . . .!" the shouts rang out from the ranks of the students.

"Wait a moment!" Mba intervened. "We want to hear what the Principal has to say first, OK? I mean, so far, officially we haven't been told anything, have we?"

"There's the Principal!" several students shouted.

From the Porter's Lodge, indeed, the Principal was coming. Only, behind him, in the same car-park where we had parked, several police trucks now pulled up one by one. They were, each and every one of them, loaded with riot-police in full combat-kit – armed with automatic rifles, shields, batons – one and all.

"What's all this?" the Principal asked presently, as he moved up to Mba.

"We're here to hear officially what happened to the Vice-Chancellor," Mba answered. "I mean, we can't be taken by surprise over . . ."

"OK, give me the megaphone!" the Principal snapped, snatching the megaphone from Mba.

By now, the riot-police had begun amassing at the Porter's Lodge, just clutching their weapons and standing there, looking on calmly at the crowd in the quadrangle.

"Listen!" the Principal began, speaking into the megaphone. "Look in the direction of the Porter's Lodge, all of you."

All glances turned towards the Porter's Lodge, and a rolling wave of murmuring and guffawing swept through the crowd.

"You see!" exclaimed the Principal. "My message is simple: go to class, or you'll have to face those chaps you see out there."

"We want to know what happened to our Vice-Chancellor, Mr Principal!" Vivi intoned. "Can he have been our Vice-Chancellor for all these years, only to vanish without even our knowledge?"

At that point, someone in the crowd shouted,"We want to know! We want to know!" And, the next moment, all the students were chanting, "We want to know! We want to know!" With the din of it drowning out everything far and near. Amid all of it, Chi moved up to where Mba and the Principal were standing.

"This is dangerous, Mr Principal," Chi said emphatically. "Send the cops away, quickly!" He gesticulated animatedly.

Across the quadrangle, the cops were slowly spreading along the corridors, slowly forming a circle around us, their guns held at the ready.

"You see, Mr Principal," Chi went on, "it's only going to inflame an otherwise quite benign situation."

The students went on chanting; chanting and dancing. In corresponding measure, the Principal and Chi went on wrangling. And in the meantime, Vivi and I had also moved into the corridor.

Presently, Vivi said, "If you can't send them away, Mr Principal, then at least let them put their guns away!"

"Fine, fine! That I can do," the Principal conceded, nodding his head vigorously.

He paced briskly to the cops, to the sound of chanting, and told them simply, "OK. Go put the guns in your trucks, then come and keep an eye on the situation!"

Amazingly, the cops immediately began trooping towards the car-park.

As the Principal walked back to us, Vivi said to me, smiling, "Right, now we're going to slug it out with them!"

"No, Vivi!" I gasped. "The guns are still within reach!"

"OK, then let's get the Principal to have the cops drive the guns right back to the police camp!"

The Principal had now joined us. At that moment, Mba snatched the megaphone away from him, and, speaking into the instrument, said to the students, "Are we going to go to class with the guns waiting for us right in the car-park?"

"Never! Never!" the students shouted. Then, as they went on shouting, someone flung an object that went shattering through the glass-façade of the library with a frightful din.

"OK, I'll send the guns away," stammered the Principal, pacing towards the Porter's Lodge again.

"Quiet! Quiet!" Mba addressed the students. "The guns are going and I believe we'll now hear the Principal on this whole issue."

Silence fell again. The cops were returning to their positions around the Porter's Lodge, armed only with their batons and shields. And, presently, one of their trucks was heard driving away.

"Right!" said the Principal, once he had returned. Taking the megaphone from Mba, he said to the students, "Return to your hostels for the moment. I'll address you on this issue at eleven o'clock this morning, in Kham Kham Hall."

"No! Now! Now!" the students responded, turning that into a chant too.

"Mba," Chi then said, turning to face Mba. "I think it's better later than now."

"OK, ladies and gentlemen!" Mba said, having grabbed the megaphone back again. "Eleven o'clock is fine. Let's go!"

And so, little by little, the students went away towards their hostels.

TWENTY-TWO

"Come to my office, Mati!" began Vivi, as the Principal scuttled away. "Chi, we'll join you a little later!"

"OK, you two," said Chi. Then, turning to Mba, he said, "Go after the students, Mba. Just make sure they don't do anything hasty, all right?"

"All right," promised Mba, jogging into the quadrangle, and following the other students.

"I'll be making a few phone calls in my office," Chi then said to Vivi and me. "No hasty measures, Vivi – OK?"

"OK, Chi."

Chi went up the corridor towards the Psychology Department, Vivi and I walked towards the Porter's Lodge, beyond which lay the Law Department. The police, in the meantime, were still standing there, at the Porter's Lodge, clutching their batons and shields.

There must have been about a hundred of them, and as we passed by, Vivi hissed, "You've had it too soft for too long, you uneducated mongrels!"

"We know you, don't worry!" said the only cop who was in plain clothes. I recognised him as one of the two undercover cops who had sat near me in the bar, on my second day at Testingtime Hotel.

"You know me? What do you know me for?" probed Vivi, rolling up his sleeves. Behind the counter, the porter looked on with dilated eyes.

I grabbed Vivi by the arm, and, saying, "Let's go, Vivi! Let's go!" I dragged him some way beyond the reach of the puzzled cops.

"You should have let me hammer that son of a warthog, Mati!" Vivi growled, punching at a pillar, as we went along.

"You promised Chi not to do anything hasty, remember?"

"Oh my goodness!" he blurted, punching with full force the

notice-board to the Law Department, and denting it beyond restoration.

In his office, Vivi said to me, "Look, Mati, I'm phoning my dad, so that he can make sure the guns don't return to Campus, whatever happens!"

"Great! You mean your dad has that much power, Vivi?"

"Ah, you know nothing about politics, Mati," he said laughing. "In politics, everybody is linked to everybody."

"Really? Well, go ahead and phone then."

As Vivi dialled his dad's number, I thought of how close the whole thing had come to erupting. And I remembered then what Chi had said of volcanoes – that they never erupt until they want to erupt.

"Dad?" Vivi was saying. "This is the situation: the students are on strike concerning Campbell. The . . ."

". . . . ."

"Yah yah! The jackals were here with their metal rods. They're still here, but the metal rods have been sent away. Can you arrange for . . ."

". . . . ."

"Fine. Thanks, Dad!"

". . . . ."

"I will, Dad!"

". . . . ."

"Fine, bye."

"There, Mati!" said Vivi, as he hung up, smiling more broadly than I had ever known him to. "The guns won't come back!"

"Wow!" I gasped.

"It's a matter of who you know, Mati. That's why Chi makes me laugh when he talks of poets legislating on behalf of whoever whoever."

"OK. Let's not start that, Vivi."

"Fine. And now, for some entertainment, Mati!" Vivi oozed with excitement, removing a steel pipe from within a pile of cartons.

"What are you talking about, Vivi?"

"I'm going out there to mobilise the students, right? I'm gonna see to it that they're armed with pipes, sticks and stones, see?"

"But you promised Chi . . ."

"I didn't promise nothing to nobody, reckon?"

"Vivi!"

"Listen, Mati, these guys've got to stop terrorising Campus, right?"

"Yah, but if you go to them with steel pipes, you're actually inviting them to Campus, are you not, Vivi?"

"As long as they don't bring the guns, it's fine. I mean, Mati, a guy's got to have some entertainment, from time to time."

"Entertainment?"

"Yah. This is what I call entertainment, me!" said he, brandishing the steel pipe.

"Vivi! Think of the students, Vivi. I mean . . ."

"Look, Mati, you and Chi, you live in the world of ideas. OK, that's fine; it's all very fine. It has worked up to now, fine. But, as you can see, it's no longer working. The cops are here, and me, well, I figure it's time to do it some other way."

"And that way is with steel pipes, Vivi?"

"Whatever you want to call it, Mati. Look, the cops have to learn to fear a University, not vice versa."

"But fighting is their language, Vivi. You can't win there, can you?"

"I'm going to, Mati!" he growled, rolling the pipe in a length of drawing paper. "You're not coming, are you?"

"Let's wait for the Principal's speech at eleven, Vivi."

"To blazes with speeches, Mati. Their time is gone!"

And then, with the steel pipe clutched under his armpit, Vivi stormed out of his office!

I lifted the receiver, dialled Chi's office number, but found it engaged. Dropping the receiver, I stared long and long at the space in front of me – and, slowly, it came back to me that a guy's got to take it easy . . .

As soon as I had got out of Vivi's office, with the door locking automatically behind me, it came into my mind that I should have phoned my brother, back in Timatami. I then began pacing towards Room P, where my cubicle was to be found.

As I passed the entrance to Room O, the most spacious of all the rooms on Campus, Chikankonz and Jah surfaced out of the room, with Chankankonz saying, "I warned you about this, Mati – did I not?"

"Yep," said I. "You can only have been right."

"And what do you say now?" Chankankonz continued.

"No more than what I've just said," said I, pacing away slowly.

Once in my cubicle, I dialled Chi's number again, and still found it engaged. On the other hand, I got through to my brother's number on the very first attempt, as had always been the case.

"Krom! It's Mati!"

"Sure, old chap," said he. "What's brewing?"

"The cupes, Krom. They're onto us, and it ain't looking too good."

"Disappear, young man. Vanish quick and swift!"

"Well, look, if you don't hear from me, you know why."

"Don't talk like that, old chap. Just beat it. Beat it quick and presto!"

"OK, keep well!"

"Take care! Remember, Mother loves you. And so do I!"

We hung up.

For some reason, my eyes just then became blurred with tears. And, wiping the tears off, I dialled Kettie's number, up at Testingtime.

"Kettie?

"Mati!" I could hear the relief in her voice. "I've been phoning you for the past hour or so. I hear the cops are down there!"

"Yep."

"Just make sure you don't get involved, Mati!"

"'Involved' is a difficult word, madam. I'll see you at my place, OK?"

"OK! I'm knocking off right now. Be careful, Mati!"

"I'll try!"

"Bye!"

"Bye!"

I left the cubicle, and headed for Chi's office. As I went past the Porter's Lodge, I noticed that the cops were no longer there.

"They've gone off to the residential area!" the porter informed me.

They had gone off to the students' residences! I began taking long strides towards Chi's office.

"Don has indeed left, Mati," said Chi to me, the moment I walked into his office.

"And guess what, Chi? The cops have gone off to the residences where Vivi went long before them."

"Oh no!" Chi rose to his feet. "Let's go to the hostels!"

"Vivi left his office with a steel pipe, and he says he'll tell the students to arm themselves similarly."

"Oh no, Mati! Let's hurry up!" Chi preceded me out of his office. As we swept past his secretary, Chi said to her, "You've been such a nice girl, Tanoza." He took her hand and kissed it.

"What do you mean, Chi?" asked the secretary. At the same time, she began weeping.

"Never mind, Tanoza," said Chi, backing towards the exit. "It was just a joke. Let's go, Mati!"

We exited as Tanoza broke into open wailing.

Once outside, we increased our pace considerably – down the steps, into the main corridor, past the Chemistry Department, past the Geology Department – and so onto the pavement that led to the residential area.

Kham Kham Hall was the first building you got to if you were coming from the teaching area. It stood on high ground, and, beneath it, the hostels spead down. And here, from around Kham Kham Hall, the police now kept watch on the goings-on, as students moved from one hostel to the other.

"All this is your making, Professor!" declared that same plain-clothes cop, as we went past them. "You and that fellow standing next to you!"

"Fine," said Chi. "And your mistake, sir, is in being on this Campus, instead of being in the police camp."

"Oh really? And who is supposed to keep order on your famous Campus, Professor?"

"Order doesn't need any guards, sir," I observed.

"Ahaaah!" exclaimed the cop. "So you also think you can criticise the police, like a White man – don't you?"

"Does he need to be White to criticise anybody?" Chi asked. For some moments, the cop nodded his head in silence. Then, turning to his men, he said, laughing, "Did you hear that, countrymen?"

"Yaah! Yaah!" his men echoed, adding, "Dissidents! Rebels! Edition!"

"Edition", one supposes, was to be taken to mean "sedition".

"Fine, gentlemen!" gloated the plain-clothes cop, now facing us. "Maybe we'll meet again, don't you think?"

"Over a glass of wine, it should be fine!" Chi said, as we walked away.

Farther down the slope, we went into the first hostel, Kham Kham Hostel I, where, at the reception, a bunch of students sat talking in low voices.

"Where is Vivi?" I asked.

"He is where only we know," one of the students answered.

"But he'll be around in time for the operation!"

"The operation?" I wondered.

"For sure!" said the same student. "You don't think we're going to sit in Kham Kham Hall with the cops surrounding us, do you?"

"And where is Mba?" Chi asked.

"Not readily available, either!" declared the same student. "This is war, Prof!" he went on. "And when it's war, it means war!"

Behind the students, past a row of dustbins, there was a pile of stones only vaguely discernible.

We went from hostel to hostel looking for Vivi and Mba: Kham Kham Hostel II, Kham Kham Hostel III, and so on and so forth. And, from hostel to hostel, we got the same answers as we had got in the first hostel. In hostel after hostel, too, we saw piles of stones, sticks and pipes hidden behind rows of dustbins.

TWENTY-THREE

When eleven o'clock came, the students began emerging from every hostel – men and women alike – each and every one of them carrying a stick, stones, a steel pipe or a chain. At the head of all of them was none other than Vivi, with Mba right behind him.

"And what do you think you're doing, Vivi?" Chi asked, as the procession came up to us, on the drive that separated Kham Kham Hall from the hostels.

"I'm heading a regiment, Chi," said Vivi, coming to a halt. "That's what I'm doing!"

Then, as the laughter cascaded down the ranks of his "regiment", he resumed the journey up the slope leading to Kham Kham Hall. Chi and I began moving alongside him. The "regiment" followed on our heels in eerie silence.

"Do you know what may come of this, Vivi?" Chi pursued, as we went along.

"Never mind, Chi," replied Vivi. "Whatever happens, I'll go down in history as the chap who put together an army in roughly one hour!"

At Kham Kham Hall, the Principal and the Registrar were standing in front of the policemen, their faces both so blank they could have served as mirrors.

"What the hell is this, Professor?" asked the Principal, as we stopped some five metres away from them.

Behind him and the Registrar, the policemen now took position, their shields and batons in the combat stance. Far up in the sky, a kite circled softly, round and round directly over our heads. And elsewhere, at the extreme northern end of Kham Kham Hall, the cooks and the cleaners stood in a tight band, looking on in still silence.

"It's gone out of proportion, Mr Principal," said Chi, moving towards Dr Dzikondanga.

"Not exactly!" exclaimed Vivi. "Things went out of proportion the moment those cops there set foot on Campus!"

"Vivi!" shouted the Principal.

"They've got to leave, Mr Principal!" said Vivi, rotating his steel pipe quite calmly. "The students are educated enough to hold a meeting, with you or with anybody else, without being policed."

That said, Vivi cleared his throat loudly. And the next thing, stones began flying from our side straight into the ranks of the policemen!

The Principal shouted, "Oh shit!" while the Registrar screamed, "Save me!" And both of them started running towards the kitchen staff.

Some of the stones began sailing in their direction, with as many hitting as those that missed.

"Oh no!" Chi exclaimed, retreating to beneath the eaves of Kham Kham Hall.

The police, in the meantime, were advancing slowly, their shields held out.

"Forget the shields – aim for their legs!" Vivi shouted.

And true, the stones began flying straight at the legs of the policemen. So the policemen lowered their shields to cover their legs.

"Forget about the shields – aim for their faces!" Vivi shouted again.

And true, the stones began flying straight at the faces of the policemen. The stones exploded on the shields with one continuous clamour, or hit the policemen's bodies with dull, deathly thuds.

The students hollered, "Hang them! Castrate them!"

The cops groaned and moaned; fell, writhed and screamed, "Call for backup! Call for backup!"

And, on the right, the Principal and the Registrar had both collapsed on a set of steps: the one with his limbs spread-eagled like a drowned man, the other doubled up against a concrete wall as though in a snooze – with the stones still raining on them as on the cops.

At that point, the plain-clothes policeman and another cop broke off from the rest, with the plain-clothes cop saying, "Let's seize him as a hostage!"

They were heading towards Chi, rushing and ducking. And presently, I scampered across the distance that separated the embattled parties, getting hit by two or three stones as I did so, and arrived on the scene just as the two cops were trying to get a pair of handcuffs around Chi's wrists.

"Why do you want to handcuff a defenceless man like him?" I asked, speaking from behind the cops.

"Whaaat?" growled the plain-clothes cop, now facing me.

"Try handcuffing me instead!" said I, putting my arms forward.

Then, as the plain-clothes cop got one cuff around my left wrist, I stiffened my arms in the same manner as my trick on Vivi all those months before. While the plain-clothes cop struggled to bring my wrists together, the other was trying to drag Chi across to the main group of cops. But Chi, in the meantime, had gripped the edge of a concrete table, and he wasn't moving. And, amid all this, Vivi came up from behind, and pounded Chi's captor right on the shoulder with the steel pipe.

The cop darted off towards his colleagues, screaming like a whistle, his shoulders askew.

Vivi moved hastily to where the plain-clothes cop was struggling to handcuff me. And, standing right behind him, Vivi tapped the cop on the shoulder and, as the cop turned around, crashed his forehead into his face.

Leaving the handcuffs dangling on my left wrist, the cop staggered backwards, only barely averting a fall. Then, with blood coursing out of both nostrils, he knotted his hands into fists, and began bouncing about, boxerlike, in front of Vivi.

"See, Mati?" said Vivi, throwing the steel-pipe onto the ground. "The moment I've always wanted!" He rubbed his palms gleefully.

"Leave him alone, Vivi. It's bad enough as it is," said Chi, who was now standing next to me.

"Watch!" exclaimed Vivi.

And then, within no more than half a second, he unleashed a whole flurry of punches to the cop's face – in all sorts of combinations, and in a sequence too swift for the eye to follow. And, like a pile of cardboard boxes, the plain-clothes cop went crumbling onto the concrete paving.

Meanwhile, the main group of cops had taken to their heels, and were heading for the teaching area. But, hot as hell behind them, the students launched the missiles thick as rain, caught up with many a cop, and crashed their sticks and pipes thoroughly upon them.

And one by one, the cops fell down – grunting and swearing, as if this was a glimpse of purgatory itself.

TWENTY-FOUR

A messenger from the Administration Block came running towards us. "The Deputy-Principal has phoned for reinforcements!" he gasped, breathing hard enough to have run halfway between here and the moon.

"Get back to your rooms, all of you!" Vivi shouted, addressing the students.

And, instantly, the students began scurrying down towards the hostels, carrying with them the batons and shields of the fallen cops. As they did so, Chi and I, preceded by Vivi, dashed across the lawn towards the teaching area.

We ended up in Vivi's office, panting like bellows, dishevelled beyond decorum.

"Dad!" Vivi puffed on the phone. "We've slugged it out with the jackals!"

". . . . ."

"Chi and Mati? OK, OK, OK."

". . . . ."

"OK, OK!"

He hung up, and panted, "Guys, there is a directive from Kham Kham to get the involved lecturers arrested, or eliminated outright. Disappear, chaps!"

"And you, Vivi?" I panted back.

"Vanish, Mati! Go hide somewhere, you and Chi. I'll arrange with Dad for your exit out of Manthaland."

We evacuated Vivi's office there and then. Sailing through the corridors, avoiding the Porter's Lodge, we reached Chi's office in a tenth of the time it normally took to do so.

"The manuscript, I've got to take the manuscript with me!" panted Chi, scooping the papers scattered about his office. In the secretary's office, on top of the typewriter, there was a note that read:

CHI,
PLEASE take care. PLEASE!
TANOZA

The offices, it seemed, were now all empty, everyone having evacuated them.

"That's one hell of a secretary you have there!" I said, as I helped Chi in scooping up the papers.

"*Had*, Mati!" Chi corrected me. "This is all over."

Even as he said so, he stormed out of his office, with me close behind.

TWENTY-FIVE

We were sailing down Kham Kham Highway, Chi, Kettie and I. We had gone past my flat to collect my passport, and to say "farewell" to Kettie. But there, Kettie had insisted on coming with us.

"We're fleeing, Kettie! The cops are after us!" I had told her.

"I'm coming with you!" she had insisted, sweeping up her handbag.

"No, Kettie!" Chi had intervened. "It's touch-and-go just now; you can follow us later, when we've gone out of the country – you and Daisy!"

But at that very moment, we had heard a whole police convoy blasting its way towards Campus, far down the road. And Kettie had jumped into the car with us.

We were sailing, sailing down the Highway. At a speed far in excess of what Chi's car was fit for.

"I told you not to get involved, Mati!" said Kettie, sniffing and weeping.

"If you're involved, you're involved, Kettie!" said I, tucking in my shirt. "There's nothing you can do about it."

"Couldn't it have been avoided?" Kettie mumbled, speaking through her tears.

"Not at all, Kettie!" said Chi, overtaking one car after another. "That's like trying to determine who you would be if you hadn't been born as Kettie."

"What has happened, has happened!" I chipped in, looking behind us.

"What has happened, has happened!" Chi echoed, shifting gear.

We had reached that long stretch of road from which you could see, without obstruction, the Campus on the right, and Zazan Inn on the left. Presently, looking behind us, I saw a huge police truck, equipped with a winch up-front, hurtling towards us as though its brakes had gone out of commission.

"The cops are behind us, Chi!" I said.

"I've seen them," said Chi. "And I'm pressing the pedal at full throttle."

"Oh, dear mother!" Kettie exclaimed, covering her face with her hands, and weeping louder than ever.

"Don't worry, Kettie!" said Chi, pressing the "hazard" indicator. "Dying is merely altering your state of being."

"Mati?" said Kettie, removing her hands to reveal a tear-ravaged face. "I wish our baby could survive, at least!"

"Well, look, Kettie," said I, stroking her hair, "Chi has said it all, hasn't he?"

"This is it!" Chi yelled.

There was a loud bang. Just one loud bang, and the next thing I knew, I was sailing through the air like a weightless pillow of straw.

I landed on my hands, rolled over my head about half a dozen times and found myself surrounded by nothing but grass.

The skin on my palms had all been scraped off, and, feeling dizzy and disorientated, I staggered to my feet like a calf for the first time. Far, far down the drift, next to a meadow, Chi's car lay on its side in a mangled pile.

"Really?" I found myself mumbling, as I slid down the slope.

"Chi! Kettie!" I hollered, as I reached the car.

There was no answer.

I clambered onto the car, my hands aching and bleeding with shattering intensity. Gripping the twisted edge of Chi's door, I struggled with it till it had come off completely, and . . .

Chi was squeezed in right there beneath the steering-wheel, covered all over in nothing but blood.

"Aaaaah!" I gasped, a cascade of tears unleashing itself from my eyes. Turning to my left, I began struggling with Kettie's door, until I had twisted it out of place.

I could not look at Kettie's broken body – one hand still clutching the strap of her handbag – the lifeless face. And as the force of it all imposed itself upon my realisation, I reeled over, and landed on my back on the ground below.

"Kettie! Chi!" I yelled, staggering to my feet again. "Kettie!"

Up on the roadside, a group of people had now gathered. They were looking down on all this as though from millions of miles away. Of the police truck, there was nothing to be seen. And sitting here, in this my exile, I cannot but wonder at the indifference of events, at that inexorable sequence in which what happens, happens anyhow – and everything else can only be in retrospect.

As I tried to extricate Chi from the entanglement of the wreckage, he opened his eyes right then, and, gazing at me unflinchingly, said, "Do not bother, Mati. My span has run full-cycle."

"Chi!" I gasped.

"We have had some sweet times together, Mati. But now I must go."

"No, Chi! Don't leave me behind!" I shouted, shaking Chi, with the tears gushing down my weary eyes in fresh torrents.

"You remember the trick, don't you?" Chi resumed, smiling that same unbridled smile.

"I do. But not in this case, Chi!"

"There're no exceptions in anything, Mati. Just take it easy. The manuscript is right next to me. Take it, Mati. Get out of the country, and tell the story of Fearfong for the wider world to hear."

And, just like that, the light went out of his eyes – as though from a lantern when the wind suddenly blows: and then the room is swallowed in a thick mass of darkness of infinite dimensions.